Peace in the Sky

Peace in the Sky

Caye Marsh

I conceived this story during many late nights nursing my first child. So, this is for my two children, who taught me what it feels like to be a mother.

CONTENTS

Part 1

Greasy gray dark. Slippery, smeary confusion.

When I open my eyes, shapes coalesce. Metal clinks against metal. I sway, suspended above the ground.

Across from me there is a shape, and I see it move. Something alive.

I don't know why but I reach up to touch one side of my head. Violent nausea. I retch, and see blue everywhere, and I can't tell which direction is up.

When the feeling fades and everything is real again, I open my eyes. It's a girl that's across from me. I don't touch my head.

The girl is sitting on the floor like I am, her back against rusted metal bars. I feel them at my back, too. She is in the dark, but I think I see her eyes moving. She is watching me.

Later, there is a little more light. A man is outside our cage, looking in. His brown cheeks are rough with a patchy beard.

He speaks to the girl. He's smiling but it's an ugly smile. He opens his pants and gestures at himself, thrusts suggestively at the girl. I look at her face, and she squeezes her eyes shut and turns her head away.

"Stop it," I say.

Both of them look at me, startled.

"Leave," I tell the man. He looks at me, both angry and scared. And he leaves.

I look at the girl, and she looks at me. Her eyes are wide now. She's waiting for me to do something.

Her long arms and legs are bony, but her face is still round and sweet. She must be young, on the cusp of her body changing. One of her sleeves is torn and there's some caked blood on her arm.

How long have I been staring at her? Three men come, their faces and arms covered with patches of calloused, horny skin. They bring water and we drink it while they talk. I hear their voices, but I can't understand them. They walk around the girl's side of the cage and grab at her through the bars. They don't come to my side at all.

I hold out my arm and say, "Come here," to her.

She looks at me for only a moment, then she scoots across the small distance between us and fits herself into the space I make for her. The men's eyes grow narrow in their crusty faces and as they leave, they shove the cage. It swings on its chain and knocks once against the wall.

The shock sends me spiraling into that greasy limbo again and when I come to, the men are gone and I'm holding the girl tightly against my side. She smells like sweat and urine. But the skin of her bare arm under my hand is smooth and tender. When I touch her, I'm overpowered by some unrecognizable feeling that sends me sliding back to the edge of that gray chasm, and I fight to stay conscious.

She buries her head in my shoulder. "Momma," she says.

* * *

I think she sleeps for a while. Maybe I sleep. I'm thirsty and I try not to drink all the water so she can have plenty.

"Why can't I remember your name?" I ask her.

"Your head," she looks up at me. "It's cracked open. What happened to you?"

I don't know. I don't know anything. "But what is your name, daughter? Remind me just once."

"Anissa."

Quietly I whisper, "Anissa," and stroke her temple. She relaxes into me. I feel her fear fading.

The men come back determined. They have poles with them that have metal crooks on the end. They pull the cage door open and reach in to hook Anissa. There is struggling and curses and Anissa cries out and I won't let her go so they end up pulling us both out. But they won't touch me. They give me a little prod with the poles, but they won't hook me. They want Anissa and they try to separate us.

I still can't understand them. I can't focus. I hear their words, but they don't seem to make any sense.

They have her now. Away from me. They are holding her arms and blocking me with the poles.

"Momma!" she screams, reaching out for me. "Momma! Call the pillars-of-flame!" They are dragging her away. "MOMMA!"

I push forward and reach her. One of the men puts a firm hand on my arm. As if in response, a needle of cold lances through my head just above my ear. I feel Anissa throw her arms about me as columns of blinding white engulf each man. Anissa and I hide our faces against each other, the roaring in our ears drowning out all else.

Just as suddenly, it is terribly quiet. My ears are ringing, and my eyes see strange after-images. There are no corpses. Three piles of smoldering carbon lay in a semi-circle around us. Above each pile there's a hole melted through the roof, the edges still smoking.

Anissa makes a strange little sound. She's quiet for a moment, then makes it again, then dissolves into laughter. Manic laughter. She goes limp. I catch her in my arms and carry her out of the building and see how crudely it's built, with stacked rocks and mud slathered in the cracks. The streets outside are rutted dirt and gravel. There are some sickly-looking trees with only a little foliage, and there are smaller huts in the distance, not far. They are all topped with flimsy hammered metal sheets. Even the parched gardens and some of the paths are shaded with them.

The sky is overcast but as I stand there holding Anissa the clouds slide by and the sun glares down. Heat breaks over me and my skin prickles uncomfortably. The squat bush at the edge of the path curls its leaves into tight rolls. I rush to stand under a metal shade and my eyes scan the area. There are miles of arid nothingness all around us. And all of it under the cruel eye of the sun.

Poor Anissa. I let her stand, but she is still weak. I breathe evenly, deeply and hold her to my chest so she can feel my calm. A ways off, there's a dip in the landscape and a row of trees. As soon as the clouds blow overhead and shade the ground, I set off across the yard, supporting Anissa. It's a long way to go and the edges of my thoughts begin to gray. I focus straight ahead and push on, step by stumbling step.

We make it. I find a spot in the shade of the trees on a ridge and look down a crumbling bank to a shallow river running orange with dirt. I take Anissa's arm and we scramble down the bank. The chalky silt at the river's margins is ankle-deep. We slog through and begin to splash our arms and legs and necks to clean off everything we accumulated in the cage.

"Don't drink it," I tell Anissa.

"It's probably what they gave us to drink," she says in a teary voice.

"Who are they?" I ask.

She looks over her shoulder up the rise. "They are the Intha, Momma, you know that."

The clouds drift by and the sun bakes us again. Anissa whimpers and we rush back to the trees. But they have curled their leaves and no longer provide much shade.

"We have to hide from it!" Anissa shades her eyes, but the light doesn't bother me. "We'll be burned."

Behind us there is noise. We squat low and turn to peer over the ridge. The sun on my neck, even in the shade, is searing. Men and women are gathering around the hut we were in. They peer inside, though they don't enter, and scan the paths around them. Their roughened brown skin and brown clothes fade into the landscape.

"Where can we go?" I whisper to Anissa. "Are we far from home?"

"Far," she says in a small voice. "So far."

Quickly I say, "It will be dark in a few hours. We can travel easier then and find a place to shelter in the day. We will make a plan, Anissa. I will take you home. Our home." I remember nothing about it, but already I'm longing for it.

She moves closer to me, both of us watching the group of Intha carefully. I hate that she is exposed to the unfiltered sunshine. I know, somehow, that it is harming her subtly. It's not just the heat of it. I have to get her away.

Clouds cover the sun again.

"Come on." I lead Anissa back down to the water.

She drinks some and I can't tell her not to because she must be so thirsty, but it floods me with worry to see her do it.

"We have to follow the river," she tells me. "That will lead us home."

I look upriver and see that in places the bank is undercut and there are shaded spots. It's not enough to conceal us for long but it's better than being in the open.

We start walking quickly against the flow of the river. When the sun breaks free of the clouds we jog until we reach the shaded bank. We squelch through the silt as long lizards slide away from us under the water, abandoning the shade for opaque water. We sit, and water soaks through our pants and wicks up our clothing.

When we're resting, I can feel just how tired I am, how thirsty I am. I'm more aware of the ever-present ache in my head that makes clear thinking so difficult, that makes the world spin if I exert myself. There are thoughts swimming around in back of the gray. But I can't reach them.

"What do the Intha want with us?" I ask Anissa.

Her eyes lose their vacant look, and she lifts her chin.

"Me, they want because I'm Riches, from the Tribes-under-the-Dome. We live there in bounty and our babies are so beautiful. You know, Momma." She smiles at me, so happy.

I'm not sure what she means by all of it, but seeing her glow with pride and love affects me deeply. I reach out to put my hand on her thin shoulder and feel an ache in my chest. Whether it is pain or pleasure I can't tell. Maybe both.

When the clouds block the light again, we move further up the river until we reach the next overhang of bank. And so on and on, sometimes breaking into a jog when the sun catches us in the open. The shadows are growing longer now as we turn away from the face of the sun so it's easier to find cover. And though we find cover, I know it's not enough. It doesn't yet show on her dark skin, but I am keenly aware that Anissa is slowly burning.

Finally, the sun is eclipsed by the horizon, and we slow to a trudging walk. We're exhausted.

"Stay here, Anissa." I find her some deep shade in the gray light. We haven't heard another person, and all we've seen is the banks on either side of us and sometimes thorny trees lining the ridge.

I walk up the ridge and scan the darkening landscape. It's so empty. There are ridges and shallow valleys and stands of scrub. There's chalky dirt, and hard-baked clay, and rocks. But no soil. And no more huts. No signs of people.

We need fresh water and a place to shelter from the sun, but I see no options. I make my way back to Anissa.

"Can you walk farther?" I ask her gently. Her head jerks up. I've caught her just as she is falling asleep.

Now that it's dark we could really cover some distance. But instead, I sit beside her and put my back to a stretch of bank that isn't so muddy. Anissa leans against me. I wrap my arms across her chest and hold her close. My legs are weak with so much walking, my throat is dry, my head throbs with the pain that never leaves me. But holding her brings peace. I bury my face in her curly hair and breathe deep. Under all the grime and sweat I can still detect her smell. The scent of my daughter.

We sleep.

* * *

I wake to Anissa shaking my arm.

"Momma? Momma?"

I force my eyes open and take deliberate deep, slow breaths. I know that I was dying, and I push away panic. I feel certain that if she hadn't woken me, I would never have woken.

I look to Anissa. Her eyes are wide in the dark and she points to something at the water's edge that's rooting through the silt with its long snout. It's like a boulder with short legs. Plates cover its humped back and a long scaly tail extends toward us. But it's not paying attention to us, so its size doesn't worry me. It's not hunting. It's foraging.

I get up and stretch and walk down to the water upstream from the animal. The animal snorts and startles. But after watching me for a moment with small black eyes, it shuffles off away down the bank, leaving deep depressions in the muck with its feet and dragging tail.

Anissa runs to me, and we both kneel and drink water. It tastes like clay and metal, but I can't stop myself drinking. I drink until I feel uncomfortably full. Anissa has finished and is touching the skin of her arms gingerly.

"Oh! My girl." I go to her and touch her softly. Her skin is so hot. I turn her and sit her in my lap and take the softest silt from the water's edge and dab it gently over her burns. I wish her clothes covered more of her. She's wearing a wrapped garment held up with only a thin strap over each shoulder. It was once red, I see, but is now so stained that it just looks dark. Underneath she has on the wide leather pants the Intha wore.

When I finish covering her shoulders with mud, she turns to me and takes my cheeks in her hands, tilting my head down until she can see my wound. She shoos away the little winged insects that are swarming it. She looks for a moment, then releases me and looks away.

"Don't let it worry you, Anissa. I will take care of it later. It's fine for now." But she doesn't say anything, and she won't meet my eyes.

"I won't leave you," I tell her. "I'll see you home. I'll see us both home."

We get up to walk again. Though we don't jog it feels like we're covering more ground. Every so often I ask Anissa to take a break and I climb the ridge and scout the area, though in the dark I can't tell much.

Hours pass by and I know dawn can't be long off. We still haven't found a place to shelter during the day.

When we stop to drink, I look up and see—floating on the surface of the lazy water—a rounded shape. I watch it as it passes. An eggshell? A few moments later, I see another. I look upstream and see a thin line of gray smoke against the dark sky.

"I smell food," Anissa says.

I start walking upstream. Anissa follows. After a few bends in the riverbed, we look up to see a shack on the edge of the bank. I start to scramble up the bank.

"Momma," Anissa hisses. "You can't!"

"Why?" I turn back to look at her.

"They'll catch us again."

"It's not the same people," I say.

"It doesn't matter! They'll know us."

Her distress is so plain that I slide back down to her.

"Anissa, you need to eat something. Maybe they won't know who you are."

"But they will," she says. "Look at my skin, Momma. They would know me anywhere. The Inthas all want girls from Tribes-under-the-Dome. Any one of them would catch me and sell me to the traders who deal in girls, too."

"Could I go alone? What will they think of me?"

She thinks for a moment and answers slowly.

"They will know you, Momma. Of course they will. Even the Intha know Peace-in-the-Sky when they see one."

"What?"

"You." She smiles slowly. "They wouldn't even touch you in the hut, Momma. They know you can call the pillars-of-flame."

I remember doing it. Strangest of all I remember it not feeling strange that I could do it.

"Can anyone do that?" I ask.

"No one!" She laughs. "No one can do that. It's impossible. Only Peace-in-the-Sky can do it."

"I'll go up there," I say, "and you can stay here."

She nods but looks uncertain. I crest the bank of the river but stay low. There's a hut with metal scraps patchworked over the roof. A fenced and shaded yard encloses a flock of some plump birds, streaked brown and gray and white. There's a dusty garden with short bushes growing red and orange and yellow fruits. I creep closer to the side of the hut and circle around back.

But behind are two large beasts that bring me up short. They have their heads down at first, but raise them, funnel-shaped ears rotating, as I come into view. Chewing slowly, they watch me carefully with brown eyes shaded by wide bony ridges. Short leathery wings are folded alongside a large hump on their back.

"Camels," Anissa whispers behind me. I turn to see her close by.

Before I can question her, she whispers, "I came to help, Momma. I know what to do." She looks so brave and determined that I don't disagree. And I like it better to have her with me.

We can hear people inside talking and moving around, and we tuck ourselves into the deep shadows by the wall. Through a small window I glimpse a man and a woman busy around a table. In the hearth burns a fire with a pan over it. There's a dirt floor, and on every wall of the hut are hung tools of cooking and of gardening, coils of rough rope and strips of brown leather, and in the corner a big metal drum.

We creep around to the door, and I raise my hand to knock, but Anissa shoves it open with a bang.

I stand startled in the doorway, and Anissa shouts out, "Behold Peace-in-the-Sky!"

Man and woman both jump and spin around, their mouths open in surprise. The man moves toward us, but Anissa stops him in his tracks with a mad tirade.

"Bow down! Bow before the godshard! Dare not touch the sacred person or pillars-of-flame will erupt from the ground and swallow your flesh! Get down! Get *down*!"

They do not get down, but they do step back, glancing at each other. I don't think they are afraid, exactly, but they are stunned. I take two steps in, just watching them, and Anissa squirms around me and grabs both plates from the table. She grabs things off the wall, too, but I can't watch her. I'm watching the man and woman.

He is broad-shouldered and dark-haired. The woman's eyes are nearly concealed by her orange hair. Their features are marred in the same way by thick scabrous patches, and their clothes are the same plain brown.

Very quickly Anissa is done, and she disappears through the door behind me. I step back slowly and note two things in the moment I am closing the door. One is the naked look of lust on their faces as they watch Anissa's back disappear. And the second is a pair of dark eyes in a distorted face, just at knee level beside the woman. A child.

Anissa is already halfway down the bank, and as I follow, I hear clanging behind us in the hut. I assume they are going to give chase. So I run, clamping down on the nausea that brings.

There's a hint of pink on the horizon which shows me Anissa's form sprinting along the riverbed. Her long legs propel her, so effortlessly athletic, that I nearly forget our pursuers and just follow, feeling joy in her health and strength.

I'm not sure how long she can maintain the pace, but my glances back show nothing but empty landscape. I don't think the Intha could run like her, they're built more for long plodding distances than fleet bursts, but our tracks would be easy enough to follow. I let Anissa keep the lead. Running is difficult for me; I have to cushion each step so I don't jar my head. I see the swirling gray at the edges of my vision as it is.

The first rays of sun come lancing over the horizon, and I catch up to Anissa in the shadow of a wide tree trunk. She has already drunk from the river and is now sitting on the ratty swath of cloth, eating the eggs from one of the plates. I drink from the river, too, and sit by her. She offers me the other plate. I take the dry, flat bread, but leave the egg and boiled greens and strip of salted meat.

The bread is thick and stale, so I chew it at length, just watching her eat. Seeing her eat so heartily eases some of my sense of wrongness at stealing.

"Aren't you going to eat more?" she asks after an audible swallow.

I look at the plate for a second and take half the strip of meat, and push the rest back at her.

"Momma, you have to eat," she says.

"You first, Anissa-my-Daughter."

"What did you call me?" she asks, reaching for my eggs with a guilty glance at me.

I pause to recall my words.

"Can I not say it like that?"

"No, that's not a word. You can't put my name in word like that." Anissa is smiling though.

"It makes sense to me when said like that. Do I use words the wrong way?"

"Sometimes. And you use words I don't know."

"How can it be true that my own daughter does not understand my words?" I ask her.

"Oh." She waves a hand, chewing for a moment. "You know different things, same way you know about calling the pillars-of-flame. That's something about being a Peace-in-the-Sky."

"You called me a 'godshard,' too. Is that the same? Am I not from Riches as my daughter is?"

"You don't remember anything?" Anissa asks wonderingly. "Really, not even one thing?"

I try to think of what I remember. But my memories are impressions, not things I can put into words. Nothing seems clear. And it makes me feel empty and painfully removed from my own daughter, so I put it aside. I watch her finishing up the food on my plate.

"Anissa, that family had a child. The things we took will be missed. Why didn't you tell me you were going to steal from them?"

There's a flash of defiance across her face.

"They stole *me* from my family, from my home, they brought me out here into the drylands to steal my babies..." She draws an angry breath to continue but I interrupt gently.

"That family did not steal you."

"What were you going to do?" she shoots back. "*Ask* them for stuff?"

"Yes."

She laughs. "That's foolish! They wouldn't have given you anything."

"But Anissa you have to give them the chance. Maybe we could have exchanged work for the food. We could have asked for shelter for the day."

"They wouldn't have done it." She sits back against the tree trunk looking sulky.

The memory of the pure greed on their faces when they looked at Anissa makes me stop pressing her. Because I think she is right. But that doesn't change the fundamental wrongness.

"Next time, Anissa," I say, "we will try to come to an agreement with the Intha we meet."

"*You* can," she says under her breath, not meeting my eyes.

"Anissa, I don't want you to do that again."

Her gaze flickers to me and away again. "Alright."

The sun is just beginning to show, and I feel the early heat on my skin. Anissa is wrapping her tender shoulders with the ratty, scratchy cloth. But I take it away from her.

"Don't put that around you." I take off my own shirt and hand it to her. I wish I had thought of it sooner. It's made of strong yet weightless cloth and the sleeves cover to the elbow.

She starts to object but then she focuses on my naked torso and freezes for a confused moment. I put the shirt over her head, and she obediently slips her arms through the sleeves. While she's busy putting it on I look down at myself, but I don't see anything wrong.

I take the cloth and drape it over her head and around her shoulders so that it forms a shade. It's not densely woven enough to completely protect her. And I know that it doesn't block any of what is most harmful. That type of harm passes straight through cloth.

"We have to find shade," I tell Anissa. I climb the ridge of the riverbed and look up and down. Behind us I look for the Intha family. But if they are following, they aren't visible to me. Upstream I look for cover and spy another hut deeper into the landscape. From this distance it looks nearly collapsed. I hope that it is abandoned.

"There's shelter ahead," I say. "Are you rested from your run?"

Anissa nods. "Should we run again?"

"No, but let's set a quick pace. The Intha may still be following. I think they can be more active during the day than we should be. Especially after all your exposure yesterday."

We begin to walk. I lead the way.

Anissa says, "I called you 'godshard' because that's what Inthas think of Peace-in-the-Sky. They think there was once one big powerful god, but he died, or broke into pieces or something. And all that's left are tiny shards. That's what they think a Peace-in-the-Sky is."

"Is that why our captors wouldn't touch me?" I ask.

"Maybe. But the main reason is because if you touch a Peace-in-the-Sky, they flame you to a pile of ashes."

She sounds resentful. It feels hypocritical to have lectured her about stealing when I have killed and the Intha kidnapped her.

The sun is becoming unmercifully hot, and we walk the rest of the way in silence. Anissa struggles in the heat, but I struggle with my thoughts. I probe the gray murkiness for something concrete and come up with only: that I can control the pillars-of-flame. But also, that it can take over for itself. So that I have to take care not to let someone touch me, grab me unexpectedly.

I listen for Anissa's steps behind me and think of her. I know—somehow I find the answer in my head—that if my daughter were to grab me, take me utterly by surprise, that I would not call the pillars-of-flame on her. Never. Never never never.

We jog the last stretch to the hut. I know Anissa's already-burned skin is hurting in this heat. The roof is not covered by a metal plate, and it's not even whole, but there's enough shade, deep enough shade, that we can hide. I'm worried about the radiation damaging Anissa, but I can't think of a way to escape it.

We settle down to sleep the day away, and I think to myself that I have to find a way for us to shorten the trip. Walking through this empty country won't work. We need to move faster, and we need more protection, and we need safe, regular food and water.

* * *

Anissa wakes me. I gasp and sit up quickly, struggling again with the feeling of having been dying. Anissa's eyes are wide and dart back and forth between my face and the door of the hut. It's full light in the late afternoon, but I see nothing around us. Then a moment later, I hear a sound. There's something coming slowly across the rocky, dusty ground.

It could be anything, a person, an animal. I stand up and walk out into the sun. It's painfully hot on my bare back.

A man is crossing the distance from the riverbed to the hut. I wait and watch him come. When he's closer he looks up and sees me and stops. He sends nervous glances to my hair, my face, my naked chest. His matted hair covers his head and shades his face, but he is looking at me with fear in his eyes. I recognize the Intha father from this morning.

We stand watching each other for a moment.

"Why have you come?" I ask.

After some hesitation he mumbles something to himself.

"Leave us," I say.

He takes a half step back and won't meet my eyes. His gaze skirts around me to the hut behind.

"Leave," I repeat.

He looks down but he doesn't go.

I go back in the hut.

Anissa says, "Momma, send him away! Make him go!"

"I asked him to go but he won't. He is only one. He has no weapon that I can see."

Anissa groans and watches the door anxiously.

After a moment it begins to creak open slowly on its leather hinges. I cannot see the man, but his view inside must show him Anissa. Suddenly he darts through and lunges for her. She screams.

I flinch, waiting for the pillars-of-flame, but no one touches me, so nothing happens.

Instead, I step between them.

The man halts. Anissa scrambles behind me and I feel her thin fingers tight around my arm.

"What do you want?" I ask him.

"Momma, he wants me," Anissa hisses.

"What do you want?" I repeat.

He mumbles something.

"Anissa, what does he say?" I ask. His accent is strange to me. I wish he would speak clearly.

"I think he wants his stuff," Anissa says.

In the corner is a pile of some of the things we took. I point to it.

"Take it. Go."

He gathers it up, but he doesn't leave. He sneaks furtive glances at Anissa.

"Don't try to touch me," Anissa warns. "The godshard will call the pillars-of-flame!"

The man retreats a few steps.

"Didn't come here to die," he grunts.

Something falls into place in my head and I'm relieved to finally understand him.

"I won't kill you," I say. "Take your things and leave us."

"Pretty 'shiny out," he says almost to himself. "Might rest away from the heat here."

"You came here under the sun," I say to him. "Already it is starting to set. You can bear it. Go."

He meets my eyes briefly and then settles back in a shady part of the hut.

"Make him go," Anissa says to me in low voice. "Get him out."

I sit down, too, keeping Anissa behind me.

"You know this area," I say to him.

"Yeah."

"Where's the nearest large settlement?"

He shoots me a strange look.

"Follow the river a bit. Cross it and strike off into the flat." He waves with his hand. "Two days maybe, then cross a ridge of rock just at the right angle, there it is."

"Do you have coordinates for any of those turns?"

A blank look.

"Will you guide us?"

"Nah. Can't be gone so long."

I lean back a little. He won't help us.

"What are you talking about?" Anissa asks. She is still struggling to understand his dialect, it seems.

"I want him to guide us," I tell her. "But he doesn't want to travel so far."

"Momma," Anissa whispers. "Those camels at his house. They're for riding, right?"

I ask the man, "How long is the journey riding one of your beasts?"

He scratches at his neck before answering.

"Might do it in a night. Long night. Gotta take some 'shine."

Anissa starts to ask me something, but we turn to him when he starts to mumble to himself.

"But can they pay, though?"

"No." I answer as if he directed the question to me. There's nothing I have. Right now, I am not even wearing a shirt.

He leans around me to look at Anissa. I resist the urge to gather her in my arms to be sure he can't grab her.

"She is not for you. Touch her and I will kill you," I say.

Anissa speaks slowly and distinctly to him. "Guide us there. We can find a trader that pays for girls. I'm Riches tribe. Worth a lot."

I'm not prepared for her to offer this, but I don't betray my surprise. The man is not so coy. He studies us both with narrowed eyes, quite obviously suspicious.

To Anissa I say quietly, in her language, "Why would you make such a bargain?"

She whispers back, "We'll wait until he gets paid. Then we'll get away. Because they can't touch us, right?"

"Anissa-my-Daughter, I may have to kill them for us to get away."

"I'll threaten them, like I did in the hut. And then we'll run."

I look at her for a long moment. She meets my eyes, her own so full of life, so proud. I am filled with admiration for her boldness, though there are so many ways the plan is a dangerous one. It's not likely to happen the way she hopes. And I'm not sure I can protect us among so many who wish us harm. I have the wound on my head to attest to that. I am not invulnerable.

Anissa mistakes the reason for my hesitation.

"Momma, that way this man will get money. It'll cover all the things we took from him and more and more. Only the traders will get cheated. And that's good! If they have less money, then maybe they won't be able to catch another girl."

"They won't," I agree. "Because likely they will die in our escape."

Anissa stares at me still. And underneath the boldness in her expression I see a hardness. Maybe she is thinking, "even better." It wounds me unexpectedly to see she's grown this way so young.

"Anissa-my-Daughter," I murmur sadly.

She turns to the man and speaks loudly again. "Don't be suspicious. Of course, we cheat the traders. But you get paid first."

He looks back and forth between the two of us and his gaze settles on Anissa.

"Make it say it won't fry me where I stand."

I realize he's talking about me.

In his language I say, "If you try to harm my daughter or myself, or separate us, or threaten us, I may. But if you treat us fairly, I will do the same for you. Take care to whom you lead us, though. I cannot promise their safety."

"Don't care about them if I get paid," he says. "That's what this Riches says, yeah? I'll get the money, even if you run off?"

"Yes," I say.

We all look back and forth among each other and it seems an agreement has been reached.

"Need a day to get the animals in order, square away my family. It's coming on dark now. But before the sun sinks again I'll be back. Be ready to start before the 'shine goes."

"If you can, bring us something to cover ourselves," I say. "And food. We have nothing."

He shakes his head. "Look after yourselves."

"Bring my daughter food, then. If she collapses before we arrive, you won't be paid as well."

He scowls, collects his things, and turns to go. We watch his back as he disappears in the direction of the river.

Anissa sighs loudly. "What are we going to eat now?"

"It's nearly dark," I say. "I will see what our surroundings offer. You can rest."

* * *

Although she doesn't want me to leave, I convince her to stay while I forage. Once I am out of sight of the hut, though, I feel a persistent tug of worry and half of my focus always remains on her behind me.

Not only do I want her to rest, but I want privacy for a necessary but indelicate task. I go through the scrubby country pulling a few leaves from every gnarled bush and chewing them. Automatically and without tasting them, I grind them with my teeth and swallow them. I grub roots from the chalky soil and gnaw them without washing or cooking them. Animals appear now in the cool dark, and I snatch lizards from rocks and crunch them whole. Always my eyes are sharp for something that Anissa could eat.

A nest. With tiny eggs. I hold them carefully in one hand and carry them back for her.

Obediently she swallows their contents raw, with an awful grimace, and we drink water from the turbid river. Then we scavenge the yard, picking over the debris left behind when the inhabitants moved. We construct a shade using the cloth Anissa stole. We hope to attach it to the animal's saddle. Back at the river I forage again for Anissa, catching a fish with my hands from which I tear strips of flesh. She tells me the taste is fine and eats as much as I can get for her. And then the sun comes on hot and terrible, and we retreat to the hut, huddling in the shade and sleeping the day away.

I try to sleep lightly so I can wake before the man surprises us, but it feels more as though I lose consciousness than fall sleep. I am useless as a guard.

* * *

"Momma, he's here."

I shake off the weight of death and sit up. The sun is setting, and two camels are crossing the dry land to us, one with a ragged rider. We get up and collect our things. The Intha arrives and hands Anissa a canteen of water and a wrapped packet of food.

We go outside in the early evening and the beasts reach down with their broad noses to snuffle in our hair. Their coat is thick and tangled. The twin leathery sails on their backs open and close slowly in time with their breathing, perhaps to cool them. We sit on a folded mat tucked into the crook of their necks. There is no way to attach the shade, so I strap it onto myself. Anissa sits in front of me, and I can tell she is excited to be traveling. She is alert and full of energy.

We don't have to guide our beast—it follows the other. Their pace is not as plodding as I would have thought. I watch the land sail by. The sun sinks the last few degrees and finally it is dark. The bright moon transforms the surface of the turbid river to silver. We turn from it at last and strike off through the stark landscape. My attention fades in and out and it's possible I sleep for small stretches despite the camel's uneven gait. We stop once or twice to relieve ourselves but otherwise travel steadily through the night.

Anissa is shifting around uncomfortably when I wake for the last time. I notice the moon has sunk and the sky is that dull gray which precedes dawn.

"I don't see any city," Anissa says quietly. "I'm so sore. When can we get off this animal?"

"Are we near?" I call out to the Intha. His beast drops back even with ours.

"Still more time," he says. "Didn't go as quickly as I'd hoped. Maybe turned away from the river too soon."

"Are we lost?" Anissa asks me with an edge to her voice.

He understands her. "Not lost. We'll get there one way or another."

Anissa looks at me pointedly.

"We don't know the way," I say to her in her language. "We have to follow him."

To him I say, "What is your name?"

"Why would a godshard care?" he mumbles to himself, not looking at me.

"What is your name?"

"Rill." He shrugs.

"Rill, will we arrive by sunrise?"

"Not likely."

There's nothing else to say. His beast takes the lead again. I pass on what he said to Anissa, who groans and tries to get comfortable. My eyes scan the horizon over and over, watching for some promising sign. Hours pass.

The sun is halfway to its zenith when I call Rill back.

"We have to stop and take shelter," I tell him. Anissa is huddled into me and my arms are wrapped around her. Our constructed shade is doing little to spare us, and the passing clouds offer only occasional relief.

"Told you we'd have to take some 'shine," he grunts.

"We've had enough 'shine," I say.

"We're close now. Another couple hours."

"We cannot be out at noon. Find us a place to pass the daylight."

He doesn't like it, but he doesn't argue. We've been traveling along a rocky ridge over which we cannot see, and he finds an overhang with some deep shade. I pull Anissa from the camel's back and carry her over. Her eyes are squeezed shut and she clings to me.

I cradle her in my lap and tip water from the canteen into her small open mouth. I feed her crumbles of stale bread with my fingers, then tuck her behind me in the deepest shade I can find, blocking any light that might reach her with my own body.

I look to Rill and he's watching us closely. He sits at the other end of the shaded overhang, but it still feels too close. I don't take my eyes from him. When I feel Anissa's body relax against mine, I know she's asleep.

"Keep your distance," I say to him.

He endures my gaze more confidently than before. His smile is not friendly.

"Get some sleep yourself," he says. "I'll keep watch."

"I will not sleep," I tell him.

"Godshards don't sleep?"

"Not in your presence," I say.

"Of course not. Godshards love best Tribes-under-the-Dome, yeah? All that about not taking sides is shit, isn't it?"

I've never heard him say so much. Something about what he says stirs some memory in me, but I can't grasp it.

"Rill, I don't have answers for you. But don't make the mistake of thinking I am helpless out here because we are far from everything."

I recall being threatened by our Intha captors, that cold, sharp feeling deep inside my mind that produced the pillars-of-flame. I reach for it deliberately this time, and find it, and keep my attention hovering over it in case I should need it.

"Not helpless? But half dead. 'Too broken to be useful. Too useful to be broken.' That's what they say about godshards." He nods at my wounded head. "But whatever did that's broken you for good. Just a matter of time now."

"And yet for now I still live," I say. "I've enough use left in me to end your life."

"Sure, sure," he says and looks away with an angry scowl.

We sit in silence. Our beasts crowd against the rocks, trying to get some shade, their leathery wings pumping continuously and stirring little swirls in the dirt. They've drunk nothing since we left the river, and I wonder how much longer they can go. Hours pass.

Rill dozes, though he wakes occasionally to check on us. He's looking down at his own hands when he speaks again. I find it concerning that he often seems to be speaking to himself though others are present.

"Following her through the world like her own little personal piece of god. No one following me. No one following any Intha."

I watch him carefully.

"Giving them all the sweet water. All the food. All of everything. A dome full of plenty. And all the children she can bear."

"Rill, you have a child," I say.

He startles and jerks around, as if he wasn't aware I could hear him.

"You have a child," I repeat.

"Oh, he's alive," Rill says carelessly. "He eats half the food, yeah? But will he ever make his own kids?"

"Intha offspring are sterile?"

He gives me an odd look. "Sometimes. Or they don't even live long enough to try. Why don't you know anything? That whack knocked half your brains out."

"I have some memory loss," I say.

He makes a scornful noise. "Maybe you remember why Tribes-under-the-Dome get paradise and Intha get shit."

"If it's so favorable where Tribes-under-the-Dome live, why don't you move there?"

"Won't let us in! Damn. You know nothing. Maybe you'll get there, and they won't let you in, broken god. Think of that? Maybe an Intha godshard not welcome there, neither."

I don't answer. I cannot reconcile what he says with what Anissa has told me. I'm her mother. Haven't I lived there with her all my life?

"Look," Rill leans in. "Come follow me, godshard. Make my family grow. Let me quicken my wife with healthy babies. Make my land green."

"If I give you babies like Tribes-under-the-Dome have, they won't live. Only Intha can survive in this habitat."

His face is contorted with anger. For a moment it seems he can't speak, and I'm worried he'll attack me, and I'll call the flame on him.

"I'm not your godshard, Rill. I'm Peace-in-the-Sky. I'm not here for the Intha or the Riches. I belong only to Anissa-my-Daughter. And I am taking us home. Guide us and get your money and be content with that. It's all I can do for you."

The day passes so slowly: Anissa breathing softly behind me, Rill restless across from me, glancing our way with hooded eyes. I'm forced to take a sip from Anissa's canteen when the sun's heat becomes intense. I feel like my flesh is baking. But my skin shows no sign of being damaged.

When night falls, I wake Anissa, and she looks at Rill and me suspiciously. It's as though she knows we talked of important things while she slept. She eats and drinks, Rill calls the camels, and we mount again and start off.

Rill keeps his eyes up on the ridge we follow. I take this as a sign he thinks we are near some important landmark, and I hope he spots it.

While we ride, my tired mind thinks about what Rill said.

"Anissa-my-Daughter, how did you come to leave your Riches tribe?"

"I was stolen! Intha are always prowling the edges of the dome, looking for girls or anything else they can get. I was visiting the trade spot in Sas Tabo just before my birthday to pick out my present." She shudders with the memory. "I was so scared when they grabbed me!"

"And did they grab me, too?"

"No, you weren't there. You were training? Or whatever you do to learn all the stuff you know. I don't know how someone becomes Peace-in-the-Sky, Momma. I wish I knew. I wish I could be one." She looks back over her shoulder at me for a moment. "Will you teach me how, someday? But not if I have to leave Tribes-under-the-Dome. I never want to leave again. Ever!"

I reach forward to cover her hands with mine and wait for her to calm.

"But we were together in the hut of the traders," I say.

"Didn't you come to get me?" she asks. "I thought you had come to rescue me, but you were so hurt I thought maybe you'd die. I didn't recognize you at first. But when you spoke, I knew I'd be safe."

I wrap my arms tightly around her. And I don't speak for a long time. Because her story opens my mind to doubt. What if she is mistaken? What if I am not her mother at all?

I close my eyes and focus. I know the girl in my arms is mine. This tender feeling—the truest I've felt—cannot be a lie. I am attached to her by some invisible force in a way that is strong and inseverable. Anissa-my-Daughter.

***

The moon begins its descent. Ahead I see a glow that is not the sun. It is lights. The town must be illuminated in the evenings.

"We leave the camels here," Rill says, dropping back. "They can't cross the rocks. Have to be back for them before light, or they'll wander looking for shade."

I pat our beast's neck as we dismount and ready ourselves to hike. I know Anissa is glad to be away from the camel, but I'm grateful to it. How could we have made the journey without them? And Rill. I watch him load up a pack for himself. He swallows gulps of water and then, surprisingly, offers me some.

"Drink up," he says gruffly. "Got to be ready for trouble. And I can refill there."

I drink deeply while he watches.

"Remember that. Haven't I been good to you? Didn't put my hand on either of you, not once."

"Thank you, Rill," I say. I mean it sincerely, but he doesn't smile.

I dismantle the shade we constructed and wrap the cloth of it around myself, looping it over my shoulders and drawing it tight under my arms. I am not ashamed to be unclothed and I do not need the protection for my skin, but it is better, I think, to be clothed more like those we walk among. We wait for the clouds to blow by and uncover the moon. We need the light to pick our way among the rocks and make our ascent.

I was worried about walking into a large town, but this settlement is not so densely populated. There are some permanent-looking homes, public squares, and shops in the town center. Paddocks for beasts and small garden plots are interspersed among the outer, more primitive huts. And at the far end of the settlement, I see larger buildings by roads leading into the land beyond. Off in the distance I see the river.

"What is this place called?" I ask Rill.

He mumbles, "What does it matter?"

Anissa and I follow him down a rocky path on the other side.

At the bottom he tells us, "We keep to the outskirts. Soon as anyone sees you there's going to be trouble. Far end of the town we find the traders and sneak up on them."

"Are they near the roads?" I ask. "Are there vehicles that run on those roads?"

"Yeah, the trucks run from there."

"Where do they go?"

"Deep into the drylands to Salvage for scavenging. Or toward the dome, to trade."

"Or to capture girls," Anissa says angrily.

"If they're stupid enough to be out where someone can see them, then yeah. They grab them."

I don't think she understands Rill's reply. "I'm sure I was here," she hisses to me.

"Then we can get back home from here," I tell her.

"Steal a truck?" I can tell she is starting to plan.

"There's a way," I say.

We skirt the town like Rill suggests. It's busy. Lamps burning some noxious substance light the pathways with a yellow glow. Houses crowd up against the shops. Despite the commerce, there's still a feeling of poverty to it. Everything is dirty and in disrepair.

Intha walk the streets and from afar I see children among them. Most of them are scabbed with the thick patches Intha have, but others have darker skin which is clearer. Not as dark or as smooth as Anissa's. But I assume these children have both Intha and Tribes-under-the-Dome ancestry, however that may have come about. It is wrong to think of Anissa as superior, but I can't help imagining what a lovely woman she will be.

Rill steals out onto the streets and comes back laden with water from a public well. We drink and drink. It feels so clean.

We near the far end of the settlement where the buildings crowd against the high ridge, and we're forced to travel the streets. Rill is so obviously nervous, I wonder if I have underestimated the danger to us. I walk closer still to Anissa, and she slips her hand in mine. We're taking her into a place where they are desperate for the money that someone like her can bring. But I trust that they won't willingly hurt her. She's valuable. I also believe they will do everything in their power to separate her from me. My hand tightens around hers.

We slow as we come to an intersection and Rill leans forward to scout around the corner of a stone building.

He jumps back and throws out an arm, sweeping Anissa and me behind him. His arm strikes me across the chest, and the familiar cold lances through my skull just above my ear. I know that I can't stop it. I'm foundering...and then I withdraw from my own body. I am within myself, flattened, dimensionless, blind. After moments of confusion, I haltingly reach out and turn off the agitated cold sliver like a switch.

And I turn and look through my own eyes again. I'm still with Rill and Anissa in the alley, my back hasn't even hit the wall.

And I'm angry.

"Rill!" I shove his arm away from me.

He gives me an irritated backward glance, but his attention is on whatever is around the corner.

"Don't do that. Don't touch me. I warned you. I can't control...I may not be able to control..."

Finally, he turns.

"Shut up, shard of a god! I'm putting myself out for you, and this rich burden you're dragging around. This wasn't in our deal, but I'm watching out for you. And you're pissing about whether I knock into you?" At this point his speech deteriorates into mumbled curses, and his scowl couldn't hold more contempt.

"I am dangerous, Rill," I say. "Don't forget that."

We wait in simmering silence as a group of serious looking men pass us. Then we proceed. I keep Anissa and myself back an extra pace from Rill. He is in a bad state, whispering angrily to himself and moving his hands like he's arguing with someone. Since seeing the group of men pass, Anissa's breath is coming quick and shallow. If I'm going to help them, I know I need to hold on to calm. Every so often I reach out tentatively for that dimensionless space, without leaving the present, and it gives me a more removed perspective.

At the next intersection we encounter a few Intha leaning against the walls. Here the buildings are more permanent, constructed of stone and mortar. We've run out of hiding places and back alleys. There's nothing to do but press on confidently. As we approach, the men stand and watch us come. I put my arm around Anissa's shoulders and pull her in tight to me. The men fall in behind us, talking low to each other. We push on, but as we proceed, we encounter more people. The twin spectacle of Peace-in-the-Sky and a girl from Tribes-under-the-Dome walking through the streets is enough that many of them follow along in our wake. Some bolder children reach out as if to touch us, but they never quite do.

As we enter a more open space among buildings, I look back to see worn clothing of faded colors, tangled red or tatted brown hair, dark eyes, open mouths showing yellowed teeth. Faces shift in and out the crowd and I can focus on none. I struggle to see them as people, but they remain a sea of faceless threats.

As we walk, more than one man falls in line with Rill, offering him money or asking him questions.

"A Riches girl and the tame godshard that follows her around," I hear him say. "Mine, and I intend to sell them. Don't want nothing off you. Shove off."

An old man we pass catches my eye, and he narrows his eyes angrily.

"Dictum 3!" he shouts in a shaky voice. "I remember! Even if you don't."

But I'm focused on watching for sudden moves from the crowd and I firmly put aside his words for later. I need to be in the present.

The warehouse that Rill leads us to has a sign outside that depicts a simplified truck, and I take it to be a shipping warehouse of some kind. It's squat and sprawling, with rocky concrete walls and a flat metal roof that seems to weigh it down. We slip under the overhang to enter at a double set of doors. The crowd we've drawn presses close behind us. So close that I pull Anissa inside to escape them before I see what we're walking into. Their voices—curious or questioning or angry—follow us inside.

The walls of the big room are lined with crowded shelves. Crates and boxes, empty drums and wheels make the space feel tight and close. The only light comes from two glaring white lanterns on a stone counter at the back of the room. There's a man leaning on the counter talking to someone out of sight, but the sound of so many people causes him to turn.

Rill rushes up to talk to him, trying to draw his attention, but the man only has eyes for Anissa. He calls for someone in one of the small rooms behind the counter, and a broad-faced, sour-looking woman appears. Her eyes fix on Anissa, and she doesn't look away. Other men appear from the door behind her. Rill keeps talking, but she ignores him. I can see that things are not going well. Why should they give Rill money? Why not just take Anissa for themselves? I can't hear any of what they say over the rising murmurings of the crowd.

I step in between Anissa and the woman, blocking her view, and I point to Rill. At the sight of me she hesitates. She nods to one of her men and he produces a pouch, briefly checks the contents, and drops it on the counter by Rill. I expect Anissa's voice to ring out and threaten them, now that they've seen me, but there's too much confusion, too much noise. Anissa and I are holding hands tightly, and I check for exits.

The door is too far. There are too many outside, now beginning to spill inside. One of the men behind the counter reaches across to grab for Anissa and barely misses as she jumps back. Rill snatches the pouch from the counter and turns as if to run. Everything is falling apart. But I can't panic.

I send my awareness inward, following the sense of that cold sliver as a guide. I pull back into myself seeking that formless space, intentionally this time. I speed the signals along my nerves so that time seems to slow. Everyone around me slows. I send my awareness outward. I map the location of every adult unknown to me in a defined radius around our location. Their coordinates appear to me, and I place a mental red mark over their signal. I enter the beam command and activate it. Around me, faster than even my enhanced nervous system can detect, white light that produces no heat appears in a blinding column around each target.

As I return myself to normal operation, I see Rill and our eyes connect. For the first time we truly see each other. The moment passes. He drops to his knees, hiding his face.

Then I am fully back to myself. I notice noise again, the roaring of the beam, screaming, sounds of panic. The ash of my targets floats through the air as we're enveloped in sudden darkness. I feel Anissa clutch at my arm with both hands.

Then it's unnaturally quiet. Anissa is choking back a few high-pitched sobs. Rill stands and looks around with terror in his eyes. We are alone in the room with the dark, smoking piles on the floor. I feel flakes of ash settle on my hair.

"Shit! Shit!" Rill sees me and recoils, stumbling backward across the dirty floor.

"I told you I was dangerous, Rill."

He runs, and I check to see that the pouch is clutched in his fist. I want him to have it.

Finally, I can turn to Anissa-my-Daughter and take her in my arms, cradling her close. For her comfort and for mine. I find a door behind the counter and stumble toward it. Inside there are a few chairs and I sit Anissa down in one. I hate to do it, but I ask her to calm down. I tell her I need her. Because the beam can't protect us indefinitely. I estimate it will need eighteen minutes to fully recharge and, even at capacity, it has a limit of thirty-two simultaneous targets. We have to get away from this town and reach Tribes-Under-the-Dome. And I need Anissa to tell me how to do it.

Part 2

"What is Dictum 3?" Anissa asks me days later, without preamble.

"You understood that man."

"Yes."

I say, "Dictum 3: to assign no preference among humans."

"So, you're remembering," she says.

"Some."

"Does that rule mean...you're not supposed to take my side?"

"Yes."

We are quiet. The heat from the floor of the truck rises up around us like a smothering blanket. Anissa drinks and passes me the canteen.

"Even if you're Momma?"

"I do not have any guidance in the case of personal relations," I say. "Or I cannot remember it."

"Are there more rules?"

"There are five Interaction Imperatives: to preserve the physical and biological environment, to preserve human life, to assign no preference among humans, to pass no moral judgment on the activities of human individuals or societies, to take no part in the organization or politics of human social structures."

Saying the words brings to my mind images of white corridors, scoured clean but worn and somehow dingy all the same. A smooth door with a placard beside it. Bright, cold lights.

I want to see more but my head pounds with pain and I let the visions go.

Anissa is still mulling over my words.

"Well, I think you try hard to do all those things. Sometimes I thought you were acting strange but now I see why."

The thought of all those terminated targets haunts me. A precious resource, destroyed. But Anissa's words are like a balm. I reach out and stroke her smooth cheek. There is nothing I wouldn't do to keep her safe. I would violate every last dictum, no matter how much it pains me.

"Anissa-my-Daughter," I whisper. The sound is lost in the noise of the truck we ride in, but she slides nearer to me on our bench, and I wrap my arm around her shoulder.

Anissa sleeps with her head in my lap. I am afraid to lay down because the vibration of the truck aggravates my injury, so I doze on and off with my back against the inside of the truck. It is little more than half full. Crates of trade goods are tethered against one side, but lax leather straps slap against the metal of the large, square container on the other. It is unpleasant to ponder whether those straps have ever bound human cargo, whether this truck and its drivers have ever transported a girl from Tribes-under-the-Dome far, far from her home.

The Intha driving the truck haven't needed to check the container behind them, so we've been safe. They were clearly in a hurry to leave the depot, before the disturbance they heard could delay them, and we've been driving nonstop every day. They are busy manning the contraption that gives it power which is nestled between the cab up front and our cargo space behind, and which apparently must be tended frequently. In the front of the cargo space, we can feel its heat radiating through the walls, so we keep back toward the doors.

To escape detection during our trip we have only to keep quiet, ride along, and sneak out at dusk and dawn to stretch our legs. Then we can feel the relative cool of the night on our faces, relieve ourselves, and bury the evidence of any food we've consumed. Then we resign ourselves to another day in the truck and climb back in. It's easier to sleep when the truck is not moving, at night.

Our fear of being found out has faded. We need the Intha to find our destination, but out here alone on the road they pose no threat to us. But I push that thought away. Finally, we have enough to eat, enough to drink, protection from the sun, time to sleep. It's hot, we're dirty, Anissa's skin is still tender with burns, and my head wound remains untreated, but we are better situated than we have been.

I lose track of how many days we travel, and although I could easily access that information by turning my focus inward to the flat dark inside my head, I do not. The trip will be over when it is over.

And finally, it is.

The truck slows and turns, and we hear the grinding of the metal-rimmed wooden wheels on rock. We jostle side to side and then roll to a stop. The engine runs down and is quiet but for the hissing of escaping steam. Yet we can still see light through the seams of the container.

"Is the truck breaking down?" Anissa asks.

"I don't think so," I say. "We've gone off road. We may be near our destination."

"Are they going to check back here?" Anissa asks, sitting upright.

We wait quietly but hear almost nothing.

I steal to the gate at the back of the truck and lift the latch. I inch the gate open, listening for any sound from the drivers. It's past noon and the white-hot sun is still glaring down. I see no one around and the road stretches out behind us, bare and dusty. I sneak around to the right of the truck and stop, stunned. Half-hidden behind low hills, a dome rises above the arid landscape. It's built of something almost colorless and networked over with the faint lines of intersecting supports. Its arching back disappears into the hazy air as it stretches away into the distance. The dome is so large I cannot see the entire breadth of it, yet somehow, it's remarkably invisible. It simply fades into the baked clay and pale chalk of its surroundings.

My eye catches on something darker showing through the hills at its base. A settlement, buildings of some sort. Without thinking, I turn my focus inward and send my vision telescoping into the distance. Details jump into view as the spot comes rushing toward me. Crude buildings shaded with metal roofs and tattered tarps lifting in the breeze. I could sharpen the focus even more, but I push it all away.

I continue around the truck quietly. The great, bright contraption that powers the thing is shuttered away, dark and quiet, and the drivers nap in the shade to either side of it. I can feel the heat coming off it even from here, and I wonder how they can bear to be so close to it. Better to be shaded, I suppose, so long as they don't cook. I see the side of the closest Intha man's face, and it is thickly encrusted with the horny skin patches of the Intha, some of the worst I've seen. What a face for a girl of Tribes-under-the-Dome to first see as she loses her home and her family forever. What a terrifying journey.

A short ways down the road I see a gate and a building off to one side. It all appears deserted. The drivers must be waiting to approach it at the proper time of day.

I go quickly back to Anissa. She is crouched by the exit, but I motion her to get back.

"Stay out of the sun," I tell her. "We are still too far to walk. There's a checkpoint but it's not open yet."

"Where are we?"

"I don't know. I saw a great dome, and a settlement beside it."

"We're home!" cries Anissa, forgetting to keep her voice low.

"Why is there a town outside of it?" I ask.

"It's a trade spot! There's a market there. You know, so Tribes-under-the-Dome and Intha can sell stuff to each other."

"Can we simply walk back under the dome?" I ask her.

"No, they control who comes and goes. I think there's a gateway. I'm not sure what it's like if you're trying to get in from outside."

"Who controls it?"

"The border crew."

I wait for her to explain it to me.

"You don't know about them? The border crews live outside the dome. They're there to keep us safe. If they see me, they'll grab me back right away! As soon as they see I'm Riches." She adds darkly, "And they'll punish any Intha trying to keep me."

"We've seen enough of that," I say.

We snooze the rest of the day away and wake when the drivers start the truck again in the late afternoon. The truck tilts and growls and bumps over unseen obstacles, and then the ride smooths out.

"We're back on the road," I tell Anissa.

We wait in uneasy silence until the truck stops again, and the sound of our engine joins the noises of others still running.

I ease the gate open and peer out. There's nothing behind us but sunset-lit road. I step out onto the rocky ground and peer around the side of the container. Our truck is in line behind two other vehicles, and up ahead is the gate, which now seems to be operating.

I turn back to the truck and lift the gate. Anissa is there, eager to get out, but I block her way.

"Wait..." I tell her.

But her eyes alight on something beyond me.

"The crews!" Anissa cries, jumping to the ground.

I try to urge her back inside, but she is leaping and waving her arms. I send my vision across the dirt expanse and see, in the twilight, men riding in a small truck. The driver sees Anissa and points, and the others stand. I catch Anissa's arm before she can take off across the ground.

"Anissa, stop. Stay here. I don't want you to run off."

I look to the Intha drivers of our truck, a man and a woman, and they are just seeing us. Without hesitation they leap from the truck on the other side and run.

Anissa's face is alight, and she's bouncing up and down on her toes and straining at my grip, watching the border crew truck approach. "They're coming!"

"Then let's wait for them," I say.

"Home!" She looks beyond me toward the dome. "Home! We're almost safe!"

The border crew, if that's who they are, arrive quickly. I cannot contain Anissa, she runs out toward them as they spill from their smaller truck. Two immediately streak off after the Intha man and woman. I can tell the border crew men are more like Anissa, long-limbed and lean, and they lope across the dusty ground and grab the thick, short Intha by their necks and wrestle them to the ground.

One of the other border crew men runs up to Anissa, and she leaps into his arms as he sweeps her off the ground, and they laugh with joy. I think she must know him.

"Awha, and who are you, sissy?" he asks.

"I'm named Anissa," she says breathlessly. "Stolen from Sas Tabo long back. I'm Riches. I want to go home!"

"Peace-in-the-Sky?" I hear a respectful voice at my elbow. The remaining border crew man ducks his head to me. "Are you traveling with them?" I pause a moment to fully understand him. His accent is different than Anissa's.

"She's with me!" says Anissa. "We hid on this truck to get back here."

The two border crew men return with the Intha, shoving them against the truck and holding them at bay using some weapon with mounted barbed bolts.

"These?" One man gestures to the Intha he's pointing his weapon at.

"Girl traders," Anissa spits out bitterly.

The border crew men nod and turn back to the Intha with a purpose, motioning with their weapons for the Intha to walk toward the checkpoint. They keep their weapons closely trained on the backs of their necks.

I watch them go and feel the weight of knowledge that we brought this on them. Did these two Intha ever traffic in people? What will happen to them, because we chose to stow away in their cargo?

A border crew man is already helping Anissa into the small truck. The man at my elbow tries to usher me along, thwarted by the fact that he cannot touch me.

"What will happen to the truck drivers?" I ask.

"Any Intha caught in company of a Tribes-under-the-Dome girl are in trouble, Peace-in-the-Sky. Big trouble." He shakes his head to shame the Intha, not to sympathize with them.

"They did not choose our company," I tell him, as I walk toward the truck where the others impatiently await me. "They did not know we were on their truck."

The man shrugs and makes some vague response, which is drowned out by Anissa urging me into the vehicle of the border crew. She sits up front with the driver and leans over the seat to hurry me along. The other man climbs in back with me and watches me shyly from the corner of his eye.

Our little truck starts up noisily with the four of us onboard, coughing black smoke, and we start off toward the dome. There can be no conversation over the clamor of its smelly engine, so we watch the road ahead. Anissa is radiant. The man beside her glances at her happily.

* * *

The border crew settlement nestles against the outside of the dome. The dome itself is like a shadowy hill, half-glimpsed in the dark, but there are lamps posted at intervals along the streets of the town. We are hustled through those streets, protected from curious onlookers, and led toward the tallest building, a big square mud-and-concrete edifice with windows of irregular size and shape scattered across its face. It looks very different from the other buildings around, which are constructed of discarded parts and natural elements. The people we pass look most like those of Tribes-under-the-Dome, but many have features and skin that recall the Intha. There are places, it seems, where the two groups mix more freely than I had first thought they might.

We are led through a wide doorway in the large building, and inside it is dark and crowded. There's a wide courtyard in the center, open overhead to the ceiling several stories up. Surrounding the courtyard, I dimly perceive a maze of small rooms and narrow corridors.

As soon as we are noticed, people begin to crowd around us. I reach for the beam switch, holding it with my mind, preventing it from being set off should I be jostled. The man with me is doing his best to hold people back. All around us are dark curious faces, everyone is talking at once, Anissa is talking loudly and happily, and nothing is being communicated.

A booming voice rings out, though, and the crowd starts to quiet and pull back. A big, broad-shouldered man with a colorful drape across his shoulders is making a path through the throng.

"Move back, move back, crew! Let me in! Make way for the boss! Let me see what you've dragged in!" His voice is loud and commanding, but perfectly amiable.

His face lights on Anissa and he peppers her with questions without waiting for an answer.

"Awha, look at this beautiful child! Are you Riches, sissy? Are you hurt? How did you come here? What are the...Shit!" His eyes light on me. "Shit, what is this? Peace-in-the-Sky? Step back, men, step back! Show some respect, or we'll all be fried."

I am suddenly the center of attention. Anissa comes to my side, and I put my arm around her. The big man looks stunned, but it doesn't take long for him to start talking again.

"Peace-in-the-Sky. Welcome! Always welcome. You honor us. Welcome back."

I open my mouth to speak but he breaks in. "Are you injured? Shit! What's happened?"

"I'm alright at present."

"Know that here we keep the Preserve for Tribes-under-the-Dome. Always. The sacrosanct, the plenitude, the prospect. How can we serve you?"

"Just see to my daughter, please. Let her get cleaned up, let her eat and drink, if you can spare it."

"For you? For you we have everything!" He gestures expansively with his arms. Everyone around us seems to echo his hospitality with their smiling faces. I am struck by how expressive they are, how mobile their faces are compared to the grim Intha.

He waves us along with him deeper into the building and the crowd makes a space for us as we go.

"Peace-in-the-Sky, your visit is very welcome, especially just now. You know our need, I guess. You know." He gives me a broad smile.

"I am taking Anissa-my-Daughter home," I tell him. "We are passing through on our way under the dome. We have not come to stay."

He turns his smile on Anissa. "Anissa, is it, sissy? Do you know me? I am Orco, boss of this crew."

"Where are we?" Anissa asks.

"Border crew headquarters at Dipol trade spot. How did you get to be out?"

"I was stolen!" Anissa says. "Inthas took me. I was out there for weeks and weeks. I went so far! Momma found me and brought me back." She smiles at me.

The man, Orco, nods slowly.

"Not taken from Dipol, of course," he says.

"No, Sas Tabo," Anissa says.

Orco makes a sound of disgust. "It is not safe there. Not safe! Here, we don't let girls into the trade spot."

He looks at me as if for approval. But I say nothing.

"Men only, or old women who've clearly taken the cure. It's just too dangerous otherwise. You should be home with your people." He nods to Anissa. We come to a staircase fastened to the inside of the building that winds its way up to higher floors.

He lowers his voice as we begin to climb. "Did they hurt you, sissy?"

Anissa looks down. "No. Not that kind of stuff, anyway."

I think of how they were treating her when I first saw her in the cage, and I hope that's the worst of what she experienced. It shames me that this stranger kindly asks her about it, and that I never thought to.

Orco brightens up. "Not many are so lucky. I will personally get a guide for you to take you back to your Riches. It will be the happiest moment when they see you again! How I wish I could be there!"

Anissa is so excited she is bouncing again and the stairs creak under her slight weight.

"And you, Peace-in-the-Sky. Are you going under the dome, too?"

"Where my daughter goes, I go," I say, though I am preoccupied with examining the struts supporting the stairs.

We come to the top floor. It's nicer up here, with painted walls and doors on the rooms which are arranged around the periphery of the building. The center of the floor is open all the way to the courtyard of the first floor, where there are many busy people around.

"Here is a room for you," Orco tells us, pushing open a door. "For very special guests. My own room is just two doors down. I'll send someone up with some water so you can take a bath. Then maybe some food. You don't want to sleep the night away, do you? Are you so tired?"

"No," I tell him. "We've had hours to rest while riding in the truck."

"Then take some time. I will send for you around midnight, and you can come see our compound. We're not Tribes-under-the-Dome, of course, but everyone here is border crew and it's very safe. These rooms up here are particularly safe, sissy, though if you want to explore you should have a guide. And don't leave the building."

"I won't," Anissa promises.

"Peace-in-the-Sky, you go where you want." He smiles. "Of course. You don't need protection. And we'll talk business later."

He leaves us and we make ourselves comfortable in the room. It's the nicest place we've been so far. There is a bed and a short table and chair. A man brings us two buckets of warm water, a piece of soap, two worn drying cloths, and a pot of something clear and slimy.

"Aloe!" says Anissa happily. "From Tribes-under-the-Dome."

We take off our clothes and Anissa hands my shirt back to me. I put aside the dusty shade cloth Rill gave us that I'd wrapped around my chest.

"Orco speaks as though he knows me," I say to Anissa.

I wash her carefully, not wanting to get soap in any sun blisters which may have broken.

"Oh"—she looks like she is thinking—"he recognizes a Peace-in-the-Sky, like anyone would."

"And they call you sister?"

"They're just being friendly. I'm not really their sister anymore because they're not Tribes-under-the-Dome anymore, not out here. But I don't mind."

I wash Anissa's hair as best I can, then pat her carefully dry and daub her with aloe from the pot. She sighs with relief and stretches her arms and back.

"Why is everyone here a man?" I ask, scrubbing Anissa's sheath and the small undergarment she had on under her Intha pants.

"They're second or third sons of Tribes-under-the-Dome," she says. "You know."

"Anissa, I do not." I hang her clothes out to dry.

"They come out here because it's hard for them to marry under the dome. But out here they might find a half-Intha wife. And there's more space."

In the second bucket I quickly wash myself, though I don't dare get water near my head injury. I rinse the shirt that I had lent to Anissa, wring it out, flap it nearly dry, and put it back on.

"They need more space because it's crowded under the dome," I guess. Any bounded population must expand until it fills the space.

"Tribes-under-the-Dome can't shelter every baby born and grown. They just won't fit," Anissa says. "That's why a woman can only make one girl. And once she does, she has to get the cure. But she can make sons first, as many as come to her. But if it's a lot they come out here, because there's not enough room."

I told Orco that we were not tired, but as soon as Anissa is clean, she slips under the blanket on the bed. At first, she talks excitedly about a pet she hopes is waiting at home for her, a parakeet which is called Hyacinth. I hold her hand until her words come slower and slower, then she is fast asleep. Later, when there's a soft tap on the door, I slip out alone.

The man outside gives a start when he sees me.

"Peace-in-the-Sky!" he says.

"Yes."

"Well, that's what Boss told me, but I've never seen one."

The man is young, not a child but still smooth-faced. "I'm Nandi. I'll guide you back to Riches after you've rested up. But Boss sent me to see if you wanted to come down."

"Anissa-my-Daughter is sleeping," I tell him, "but I would like to see Orco again."

"I can take you." Nandi seems to wear a perpetual half smile, like he's anticipating something amusing.

I follow him down the staircase and he keeps glancing back at me.

"I thought you'd be taller. You're short as an Intha."

"I hope you've been told that you cannot touch me," I tell him.

"Oh yes, loud and clear. I'm the respectful type, anyway."

"It's not out of respect. It's for your safety."

"Oh, I know. The pillars-of-flame. Coming down from the stars." He gives me a wondering look as though he'd like to see it.

"Anissa believes it erupts from the ground," I say.

"Boss says it comes from above," Nandi says. "He knows about things."

I nod. That is why I want to see him.

* * *

Orco is talking to other people, directing loudly something being arranged on the first floor of the crew's building, but when Nandi leads me up, he excuses himself.

"Come with me," Orco says, arching his arm like he would wrap it around my shoulder, but not quite letting it land. "I don't like to have you out in the press, you know." He gives me a knowing look. "Too dangerous."

"You don't like things that are dangerous," I say. He's said those same words before.

"No. I keep it safe here. That's my job." He smiles. He's led us to a corridor with less traffic. There are three rickety chairs in one of the turns, and he sits expansively in one. I perch on another.

"Aren't I dangerous?" I ask.

"Yes, yes," he nods. "But your advice? Worth everything."

"Orco, I do not remember you."

"Awha, no? Well, I don't expect such a thing. You must meet many, many people." He motions to a passing group to continue by.

"My injury has clouded my memory." I pause for a moment, but I want to trust him. I've seen his kindness to Anissa. "I have felt very lost here, since I regained my senses. I know almost nothing about this place."

His dark eyes are warm. "How were you hurt?"

"I don't know."

"Whoever did it fried for it, I'm sure. I thought it would be impossible to do that to you! I suppose maybe if they ran up behind you and hit you with a single blow? But who would dare? Who would dare?" He threw his arms up like it was incomprehensible.

"Also," he added, his voice quiet, "it looks very bad. Very bad. Will you survive it?"

"I have so far," I say.

"Well, I hope you continue to thrive, Peace-in-the-Sky!" He gives me a wide grin.

"Thank you."

"And you have a real interest in this Riches girl. She must be special. She must be part of some larger plan, for you to take an interest?" He gives me a private smile.

"She's my daughter," I say.

And now he gives me the same non-committal look and polite nod I've seen him give me several times since we've arrived.

"You doubt me."

"What you say, I believe," he says, holding up his hands.

I look him in the eye steadily. His smile doesn't fade, but the moment is tense. He stands up.

"Please come with me," he says.

Just down the hall there is a door that he pushes open, and waves me inside. I step through the narrow doorway and see a person standing at the back of the small room. When I move, the other person moves also.

It is my reflection.

What surprises me most is that she does not look surprised. Her face is a peaceful blank mask. She is short and her skin is dark. Her hair is white. Not the curled, wispy white of an old woman's hair, but short and straight and thick and unnaturally bright. And the eyes. Violet, oddly reflective.

I watch myself reach for my arm and feel it. It is flesh, warm and alive. I take a deep breath and feel air come and go from my lungs. I make myself aware of my heartbeat. I blink my eyes and curl my toes. I turn my head and get a glimpse of the wound in my head. But I shy from examining it too closely. What's done is done, and I'm certain there's nothing anyone here can do to aid me. But I do not know how I know that.

I feel confusion and distrust and unhappiness and none of it plays across my face.

I step back out of the doorway.

Orco is there looking at me.

I know why he showed me myself. I look different from everyone else I've seen.

"You've seen me before," I say.

"Yes, though you looked different then. Devan, the man who was boss before me, showed you to me when you visited us long ago. I've heard other stories, too, and the descriptions are always different."

"Then how do you know it's me?"

"That hair," he points. "From miles away I'd know that colorless hair. And close up, well, who else has shiny purple eyes? No one. Now you're walking around looking a little like Riches with that dark skin, but I saw it brown like the Intha and heard of it looking pale as chalk."

"What makes you think I'm the same person as those others, then? Maybe there are many of us." I feel as though there are many of us. Or, at least, there were.

"I don't know. But only you come down here."

I pause for a moment.

"Come down here? Down?"

He shakes his head. "You're the one who knows everything. Now you're asking me questions. But you never explained it to me."

I just look at him.

"I have so many things to talk with you about, Peace-in-the-Sky. Just let me get some things ready. Make yourself at home here, please. Anything you need just ask for it. I'll send for Nandi, and he'll show you anything you'd like."

"No," I say. "I'll go back and sit with Anissa-my-Daughter until she wakes."

"Then I'll have Nandi bring you some food. Get some rest. Maybe you can start to heal? If there's a way I can help, I will. Nothing would please me more." He sends me away with a broad smile and a wave. "I will see you soon."

* * *

I start back alone, fighting the aching in my head as I try to remember. I make it to the base of the stairs before Nandi catches up to me.

"Need anything? Let me walk you back," he says.

"You said you've never seen Peace-in-the-Sky," I say, "but I've been here before."

"One time, but that was before I left Tribes-under-the-Dome. Before I was born, even. Not many people see Peace-in-the-Sky twice in their lives. Most people don't even see you once!"

He follows me up the stairs, and at the top I see Anissa peeking around our door. She smiles when she sees me, and I feel some relief from the confusion of before. Her happiness clarifies my purpose for me, time and time again. I examine her features closely as I grow near, comparing them to what I saw in the mirror. But it's hard to compare a youthful, smiling face to a grown face that is forever calm and still.

Since Anissa is already awake, Nandi takes us to the hall where everyone eats. It's crowded and loud and hot, but the food smells good and we pass many smiling, curious faces. Anissa basks in the attention, pulling herself up tall with a raised chin. She is young and strong and beautiful, and she knows it, and I am happy in her wake, admiring her as much as those in the hall. I remember what Orco said about it being dangerous to have me in a large crowd, so I steer Anissa to a spot at the end of one of the long tables, close to a wall. Nandi sits down between us and the rest of those at the table. He seems proud of his role as escort and protector.

Plates are brought soon, the same food for everyone in the hall.

Anissa looks at hers with a little sigh of disappointment.

"No avocados? Mangos?" she asks Nandi.

He laughs. "We don't eat like that out here, sissy. Food from there almost never escapes. There's barely enough in there for Tribes-under-the-Dome. Why do you think me and all my brothers are out here in the first place?"

As we eat the cactus spears, wilted, bitter greens, and strips of cured meat, Anissa asks Nandi, "What tribe are you from?"

"Sante," he says. "Most at Dipol are. Some from Pepper. Almost no one from Riches or other Tribes-under-the-Dome. They go to Sas Tabo or Chimiminga trade spots."

I listen to the names gratefully. Hearing them stirs the muddy swirl of my memory.

We finish and send our plates back to the kitchen. Anissa wants to walk around and see things, so Nandi takes us on a tour. The crew's job is to defend the dome's borders and the trade spot, so there's rooms with maps, rooms with stored weapons, rooms with goods confiscated from the Intha, now being re-purposed. There are sleeping rooms and washing rooms and two kitchens and a laundry. Everything you would expect in a building meant to house many people.

Nandi shows us a large room with benches lined up in front of a raised table.

"We keep the Preserve just as we were taught," he says to me with a smile.

I understand him to mean that many people gather here to practice a religion.

"The sacrosanct, the plenitude, the prospect," Nandi murmurs as we leave. Archaic words with no real meaning in this dialect.

Next, we see a large bay where trucks are stored and repaired.

"You don't use the same heating device the Intha power their trucks with," I remark.

"No, we're not steam powered. We use fuel-burning engines. It's tricky making it but we can drive our trucks when the sun is down. Very useful." Nandi smiles. "You taught us, they say."

"I don't see the truck we came in," I say.

"No, we can't keep it. Too valuable to the Intha. We'll trade it back to them."

"You give it back?" Anissa asks angrily.

"Have to, sissy. Those engines of theirs are so important to them, they would get violent if we kept them. But we can ask such a high price, and because they used it to steal girls, they can only grumble, really."

"They'll just use it to steal more girls!" Anissa says. She is almost shouting. I put my hand at her back to calm her.

"They use those trucks for all kinds of things," Nandi says. "And they can't actually steal many girls. We make them almost impossible to get."

"Nandi is not the one who decides policy," I tell Anissa. "Talk to Orco if you are unhappy with it."

"Because you won't!" she says to me. "You won't take sides."

"Anissa-my-Daughter..."

"I want to go home!" she says, suddenly wilting. "I want to go home, Momma. When can we go?"

"Let's go back to our room," I say. I nod to Nandi, and he starts off down another corridor. Anissa follows along with her head drooping.

Back in our room I settle her on the bed, and she curls up in a ball. I pat her hair until she begins to relax.

"I will talk to Orco," I tell her.

"About the truck?"

"About going home. I can discover when we leave and how we can best prepare. Once we know when we're going the waiting won't seem so bad."

Anissa nods miserably.

I open the door to find Nandi.

"Is there something she can have to do? Something to look at? A way to pass the time?"

He disappears and returns quickly with some dice, a sort of peg game, and some small, whittled figures with scraps for clothing.

I take the things to Anissa and try to interest her in them. Then as soon as I can, I slip back out to Nandi.

"I want to see Orco," I say. I follow where he leads.

* * *

"Peace-in-the-Sky!" Orco booms when he sees me. "Very fortunate you come when you do! I was going to send to see if you were free."

"Are you ready to send us home?" I ask.

"Surely you would rest some more? Your girl is not ready to travel just yet? And I have to arrange it, you know. Get the permission chips. Come with me, come with me. We can talk."

He waves Nandi away and leads me down a crowded corridor on the ground floor. To my surprise we approach an exit, and there's a car waiting there. I step out into the night, which is well-lit from the lamps now burning brightly. The car takes us through the narrow passageways of the settlement, which are busy with people, and out toward the silvery edge of the dome itself.

I watch with wonder as we draw nearer. It's beautiful. An innovation far beyond anything I've seen in my travels, and yet it feels ancient. It stretches up and out and away from us, nearly blotting out the sky. It doesn't obscure the horizon; it is the horizon.

Orco is not as impressed as I am. He steps out of the car just a few strides from the wall and looks at it with disgust. The driver of our car cuts the engine, and Orco gestures to the cloudy material that forms the sides.

"Now, dearest Peace-in-the-Sky. Here's what we face. What can we do? The rat problem inside grows and grows, and soon we will have safety problems as well. Already the crews talk about organizing patrols to watch these areas during the day. The day! Because the Intha could be out in their solar trucks at some spot we cannot even see from the trade spots, working their way inside."

I look more critically at the structure of the dome. The surface of it is so abraded that I cannot resolve anything inside, I only get a vague impression of dark shapes.

"It's cracked," I say.

"Yes, it's cracked!" He waits for a moment. "But how can we repair it?"

"You might patch it or block it somehow. I don't think that you can repair it," I say.

"No, not a patch!" He shakes his head. "The Intha will just rip that away. But you can teach us how to really fix it. To make it new once more. You built it, after all."

I look at him. Although I feel surprised, I know now that he cannot see it on my face.

"I did not build this."

"You did! Peace-in-the-Sky did. And you always have answers for our problems. This one? This is a big problem."

I look at the dome silently.

Orco says, "I thought perhaps if we heated it somehow, and got a lot of sand in the melted parts to seal it up? Is that how it's made, with melted sand? Like lightning strikes in the desert."

"No, it's not glass. It's a metal-fiber-reinforced polymer."

"Awha, you see! You do know," he says. "This crack is small. I can show you some of the bad ones if you will travel."

"There's no need," I say. "Orco, I cannot repair this. Anissa and I need to get back under the dome. I need to take her home."

"Let me send her home, then. But we need you out here, Peace-in-the-Sky. Otherwise, how can we keep Tribes-under-the-Dome safe?"

I say, "I will not be separated from my daughter. And I hope that the people inside will remain safe despite the cracks. The dome overhead still protects them from the sun's rays."

Orco's expression grows dark.

"I'm not talking about exposure. I'm talking about maintaining the Preserve! That is the problem. Wasn't it you who taught us the Preserve is 'the sacrosanct, the plenitude, the prospect'?"

I recognize the words from Nandi's benediction. And without considering how it's possible I search the terms. Sacrosanct: not to be trespassed upon. Plenitude: full or complete. Prospect: expectations for the future.

I'm aware of Orco watching me. His expression shifts from glowering to worried.

"Peace-in-the-Sky, you must be broken yourself," he says. His eyes scan to my open wound.

"I don't recall teaching you those terms," I say.

"Awha, I can see that you remember nothing," he says. "The damage is as bad as you said. I just couldn't believe you." He taps his finger against his lip and frowns. "But how can I fix you?"

"You can help us," I say, "by sending Anissa-my-Daughter and me back home. She doesn't want to wait."

"She?" he says, and lifts an eyebrow. "Does she command Peace-in-the-Sky?"

"I want to take her home," I say.

He laughs. "Then I will work on it. Faster, just for you."

"Thank you," I say, though his tone carries a hint of teasing and I'm not sure if he is serious. "I'm sorry that I cannot help you with your problem."

"Awha, but I will ask again," he says, ushering me back to the car. "When you start to remember."

I don't want to be caught up in these problems, I want to continue my journey with Anissa. But the engine of the car starts and conversation is no longer possible.

* * *

I return to Anissa and Nandi accompanies us to dinner. Orco joins us for a while, too, and adds to our interest so much that we can hardly eat for people crowding around to try and talk with us. When he leaves, we finish our dinner, then sit. Everyone lingers over dinner, and Nandi chats with friends. He introduces us with a hint of pride, calling Anissa 'sissy.' Many of those who are introduced to me nod and murmur the Preserve benediction and smile. Some reach out as if to take my hand, but catch themselves and just smile and nod again. Then gradually the crowds begin to thin.

The sky is graying, dawn is coming. I walk Anissa back to our room, supporting her on my arm. She is pleasantly sleepy. We are just walking through our door when I hear someone behind us. It is Nandi.

"Boss wants you, Peace-in-the-Sky," he says with his customary smile.

"Now? We were just speaking with him. Anissa-my-Daughter, wait for me. Lay down. I'll be back soon."

She waves drowsily and sits on the edge of the bed. I follow Nandi down the hall.

"What does he want?" I ask.

Nandi shrugs. "Didn't say."

Instead of walking down the stairs, though, we cross to another room on this floor. Inside is a wooden ladder leading up through the ceiling. I hesitate, but Nandi waves me up.

"Boss is up there," he says cheerily. "Go on, if it holds him, it'll hold you."

The flat roof of the building is covered with a thick layer of grit and sand. There's a breeze. It's cooler than I expected. Above me the sky stretches endlessly in all directions, dark and speckled with pinpoints of light. In the East glow bands of pink and gold, streaked with gray-blue clouds.

I almost don't notice Orco, though he is the only thing up here besides myself.

A big gleaming smile shows on his dark face. Looking over his shoulder, he holds out his hand to me and I join him on the edge of the roof. I can tell he means for me to stand closer, but I keep a space between us.

"I like you like this," he says. "Small and dark. It suits your only mood."

"My personality was the same before, then?"

He laughs. "Awha, yes it was."

"Why are you up here?"

"Looking at the sky. Pretty isn't it?"

"Beautiful," I say.

"I want to show you something that can be seen this time of day, this certain time of year. Do you know what I'm talking about?" His normally booming voice is quieter, though still as rich and warm as ever.

"No."

"How strange. Last time we were up here, you showed me." He steps closer and puts his arm around me.

I arm the switch.

But he doesn't touch me, his sweeping arm directs my attention upward. My eyes scan the sky, but I see nothing.

"That little twinkle, you see it?" He points, his hand close to my cheek. "A little silver spark..."

I do see it. A flash of silver close to the horizon. Not a planet. Not a star. Something reflecting the rising sun. Too far away for even my aided sight to resolve.

"What is that?" I ask, not expecting an answer.

"A station in low orbit," Orco says. "Your words. I can't understand such a thing."

I glimpse the white corridors again, flooded with bright colorless light. Doors that slide open and air-lock behind you, numerals incorporated into the walls to tell you what deck you're on because they are all the same...

"Are you alright?" Orco asks.

I bring myself back to the moment and turn to look at him. I am uncomfortably aware of his muscular bulk compared to my own small build. We are standing closer than I remember.

"Does that stir up some memories, Peace-in-the-Sky?"

"Some," I say. I wish he wasn't talking so I could focus solely on what is running through my head.

"You'll remember. More and more. I can help you. And then together we can solve all our problems..."

I am ignoring him, my mind racing, until I feel his thick fingertips stroke the back of my shoulder.

I jump away from him. "Are you mad?" I ask angrily. "Consider not only yourself, but those on the floors below you!"

"Awha, you weren't so cold before! The last time we stood on this roof."

I am stunned.

He continues. "You say that Anissa is your daughter. If that really is true, then who is her father? Have you thought of that?"

He holds his hand out to me. But I don't take one step in his direction. I send my thoughts racing, looking for some evidence...

"Peace-in-the-Sky," he says quietly.

"Stop interrupting me," I say. "I need time to think. Thank you for showing me the station." I nod to the horizon. The sky is brighter now, and the silver flash is no longer visible. "Good night."

Orco does not follow me. As I descend the ladder, I remember Anissa is waiting for me. I nearly collide with Nandi as I leave the room with the ladder in it.

"Whoa!" Nandi holds up his hands, smiling. "Did Boss make a wrong move?"

"Why did you wait?" I ask curtly. "My room is just down the hall."

Nandi laughs and falls in behind me, stepping quickly to keep up. But before I reach my door I slow and turn to face him.

"How old are you, Nandi?"

He shrugs. "Twenty, maybe?"

"Thank you. Goodnight."

I slip into my room. The light outside is brightening but in here, it is dark and still. Anissa is asleep on the bed, her clothes still on. I shift her toward the wall and slide in beside her.

"Momma," she murmurs, sliding her thin arm across me.

I wrap my arms around her and relax into this welcome touch. If I had ever felt so close to someone else, wouldn't I remember it? The way I do with Anissa?

"How old are you, Anissa-my-Daughter?" I whisper.

"Ten," she says.

And, according to Nandi, whom I believe, I haven't visited here once in his twenty-year life. I thought so.

* * *

I sleep as deeply as I always do. It's Anissa who wakes me as she shifts position in bed and digs her elbow into my arm. She is asleep again after a moment, but I lie awake. I can feel that night is coming on. The heat of the day is fading. If we are to go under the dome, we must switch our nights and days again. I am determined that we'll leave during the next daylight cycle. I had better warn Nandi so he can prepare.

Nandi arrives and we three go to breakfast. It is not so crowded as the other meals, and thankfully Orco does not appear. I encourage our group to eat quickly, and when we get back to our room, I send Anissa inside and stand in the hall talking with Nandi.

"Where can I take you today, Peace-in-the-Sky?" he asks. "Boss will send for you later, maybe, but we can go wherever you want until then."

"I've seen enough. It's time to go back under the dome. We leave as the sun rises, Nandi. You should get some extra sleep today if you can."

Nandi's smile wavers and his eyes slide from mine. It's only a moment, but I recognize instantly what it means.

"You've been told not to lead us away," I say.

He holds up his hands. "Oh no, I will! But, awha, Boss says when."

"Orco does not intend for us to leave," I say. But as I say it, I realize it's only me that Orco wants to keep. I could send Nandi to take Anissa home and he might do it.

"Nandi, we are leaving. Anissa-my-Daughter is homesick, and we have spent enough time here. You must make a choice whether to trust me and be our guide, or to serve your boss."

He looks surprised.

I say, "Remember who I am."

Nandi looks at me intently, and I feel as though he's searching for something in my face. Which I know to be utterly blank.

I hold out my hand.

He looks down at it, then back up at me with a question in his eyes.

I extend my hand farther.

He takes a deep breath, and reaches out slowly to take it. I shake his hand. He laughs nervously and glances upward.

I drop his hand. "If I had called the pillars-of-flame, you wouldn't have time to look for it," I say. "Be prepared to go at dawn. What can we do to help you prepare?"

"Awha," he runs a hand over his short hair. "We'll take a car. I can get a key. I'll take some food for myself. I can't take anything from Tribes-under-the-Dome. You can do anything you like, I expect." He smiles at me. "That's it. What else do we need? There's water everywhere in there. Skito balm! I'll get some."

I can tell by the way he's speaking that he's nervous. But I hope that he won't tell Orco what we're planning.

"If you think of anything else that we can help with, come find me, or tell Anissa and she will relay it to me," I say.

He nods. Then he smiles a big smile. "I'd better go. Gather stuff slowly, throughout the night."

"Get some sleep, too," I tell him.

"I will, I will." He waves to me as he turns away down the corridor.

I return to Anissa and play the dice game with her. She enjoys it and I watch her smile and laugh with satisfaction.

"We're going, aren't we?" she asks.

"Yes. I've talked to Nandi. But we are leaving without Orco's permission so do not talk with anyone about it."

"What? Why would he want to keep us?"

"He wants my help," I say.

"Well, you can stay and help him," Anissa says easily.

My hand stops in the act of throwing the dice.

"Because it won't take long and you'd come along right away, afterward, right?" she adds.

I throw the dice.

"No, it is not a problem that is easy to fix," I say. "And I don't want to send you alone with Nandi into a place that I don't know. Or don't remember."

Anissa says, "I'd rather have you with me, anyway."

* * *

When Nandi comes to get us for lunch, he tells me that Orco wants to see me afterward. As we walk down the halls he admits—and I can tell he's been instructed not to tell me—that Orco has a trip planned for me. A small group is to go out in a truck and they're taking some supplies so it will probably last the remainder of the night.

After lunch I tell him to escort Anissa back to our room and to stay with her. Watch over her. Then I ask him how to find Orco. He seems anxious letting me go on my own, but I tell him I can find my way, or ask anyone along the way.

When he and Anissa are out of sight, I follow his directions for half the way, then turn and walk out of the crew's building using a different exit. There are many that see me, but everyone only smiles or waves.

It's nice to be out on the streets. There's a breeze and people of all kinds to watch. Here they live better than the other places we've been. They're wearing bright clothes and eating street food with their hands and laughing or arguing.

I see a group of dirty, rough-looking Intha men walking down the middle of one street. They're looking around them defiantly, and the crowd parts for them a little. The tall border crew men look down at them with some hostility, but there's no fights. And half-Intha women and children are everywhere.

I want to see the trade spot itself. I ask a couple I see walking together. But they don't answer me, they just stare.

"What are you?" the man asks.

The half-Intha woman looks from me up at her man with wide eyes.

"A godshard," she hisses to him.

"Awha, that's true?" He looks at me. "Peace-in-the-Sky?"

"Yes," I say.

They both stare at me a moment more and another man walks up to us.

"Peace-in-the-Sky?" he asks.

"Yes. I'm looking for the trade spot."

"I'll take you!" A little boy who's been listening to us runs up.

"Don't touch her!" the woman warns him.

"I know, I know," the little boy says. "Come on, godshard. Follow me, follow me."

So, I do.

"You have a scripp for me?" he asks, as we walk briskly along.

"What is that?" I ask.

"A scripp, a scripp! So I can buy in the market." He bounces impatiently.

"No. I don't have anything."

"Don't matter, don't matter. I tell my friends: godshard following me around the market!"

It's a pleasure to follow his quick steps through the crowd. He glances back at me every so often, smiling to show crooked teeth.

"This is close enough," I say when I can clearly see the dome's edge and some high gates obscured by a crowd. "I'll find my way. Thank you for your help. Go find your mother, now."

"Mam's busy," he says. "I go and tell Moggi! He won't believe me. Now he got to let me play in the third!"

The gates to the market are heavily guarded, and there's a long line waiting to get in. No one gets in easily, no matter what they look like. No carts are allowed through, it seems, so everyone waiting has a heavy pack on his or her back, piled high with wares. Two Intha directly ahead of me are carrying racks with pots and pans and wooden spoons lashed to them.

It's hot in a crowd, even at night, and everyone waiting looks tired and frustrated. I walk to the front of the line where four guards are searching merchants. Two other guards stand by the entrance, holding long wooden poles with sharp metal tips. Each one has a bolt-throwing weapon hanging from a wide belt.

The market behind them is walled off with big sheets of repurposed plastic and metal. There is no way to see inside without entering. The market is attached to the side of the dome and there must be an entry into the dome inside, but I cannot see it, and I cannot see an easy way to get through that way. I was hoping I could take Anissa and simply talk my way through, but it doesn't seem likely. There's nothing to do but return to the border crew. I hope by now that Orco has left on his trip without me.

I take an indirect route back and simply watch the people around me. Many of them stare back, with curiosity or fear or interest in their eyes.

The building of the border crew is dark inside after the lantern-lit streets. It takes me a few turns to orient myself and find the way to our room. Nandi stands outside, still guarding Anissa after my instructions hours ago. I am pleased with him.

"Are you ready for the morning Nandi?" I ask, as I step past him and open the door.

The room is empty.

I round on him and cut off his answer. "Where is Anissa-my-Daughter?"

"Awha, she's with Orco..."

I stride down the hall and Nandi hurries to catch up.

"She's fine!" he says.

"She's a hostage," I say, not looking at him.

At the bottom of the stairs, I pause. He stops, too, and I say, "Take me to them!"

He starts off at a lurch and I'm close behind him. We wind through corridors until we come to the vehicle storage room, the bay door opened onto the small hours of the night. There's a small crowd there. Orco is balancing his bulk on a chair and Anissa sits beside him on the ground. Behind him stand several men loosely holding long pikes. There're other men, young and old, gathered around, too.

Orco is telling a story, his arms fly out in animation of his subject, and everyone is watching him and smiling and nodding along. Anissa looks happy and unharmed. I slow.

I walk between two of the larger trucks and emerge into the group across from Orco in his chair. Nandi is close behind me. But I feel more his anxiousness than his support.

Orco stops talking when he sees me and smiles, waving me over. I stay where I am. Anissa stands up to come to me, but Orco wraps his hand around her arm.

"Let her go, Orco," I say.

He releases her and wraps his arm around her shoulders, instead. A gentler hold.

"Come over and let's talk," he says warmly. "Goan, pull up a chair for her."

"We're leaving," I say. "Nandi, get the truck ready."

Nandi shifts from foot to foot.

"Why won't you speak with me, Peace-in-the-Sky?"

"I have nothing to say to you. Thank you for your hospitality. We're rested and now it's time for us to leave."

His wide smile looks strained. "You are not yourself," he says. "Let me send Anissa here back to her family. Nandi will take her. Nandi, get the truck ready. Go on."

After a shuffling pause and a glance at me, Nandi heads for a truck.

"You cannot keep me here against my will," I tell Orco.

"Why won't you come over and talk with me?" he asks. He stands up from his chair.

Anissa looks up at him with worried eyes.

"Let me go," she says.

"Tell Momma to come and have a little talk. I have to shout just to have a simple talk."

"Momma..." Anissa's voice is worried.

I walk half the distance. The men holding pikes circle around to my sides. They still seem relaxed and their hold on their weapons is loose. I see no one carrying a projectile weapon. With the exception of Anissa and Nandi, I have everyone in the room targeted. I see them simultaneously as people in the room with me and as dark spots on a map with red hashes over them.

"Orco," I say.

"Will you fry us all?" he asks, his tone light.

"No. I will take Anissa and go."

"Come get her, then." He drops his arm from around her shoulders and she stumbles to me.

I take a few steps to catch her, but Orco moves quickly and catches my arm in a tight grip just as one of his men shifts forward and sweeps Anissa away. He pulls her back among the trucks, but waits there, watching Orco and me.

I look at Orco's fist tight around my upper arm. No one has ever touched me like that before. It's painful and intrusive.

"You see?" Orco says. "Just as I thought. You cannot call the pillars-of-flame." He tilts his head and taps his finger against it. "You're too damaged." He smiles.

I retreat inside myself and speed the impulses along my nerves. Everything seems to slow, and I reach out, trying to target the vehicles around us. But I cannot. I can't target inanimate things. One of the trucks near us has some grain spilled in the bed of it. I can smell it. And gnawing those grains, oblivious to the people around them, are a handful of rats.

Blinding light fills the room and men scream high and fearful. Pikes clatter to the ground and men fall to their knees, their arms above their heads.

Orco bellows and jerks me off my feet. I bite down and taste blood, so strong is the effort of blocking the switch that would terminate him.

Dust settles. The truck beside us smokes with a metallic stink. The rats are now a scattering of ash across a truck bed.

My vision returns to normal, and I see all around us men are falling back from us. The man who held Anissa has released her, and she crouches near a truck, watching me anxiously.

Orco lifts me to my feet.

"You cannot hit me, I am too close," he pants.

"False. Only my mercy stands between you and oblivion, Orco."

He is breathing fast and his eyes are struggling to adjust to the dim light. His gaze darts around the room but I can tell he's not able to make sense of what he sees.

"What can you possibly gain from antagonizing me?" I ask.

"We need your help," he says, and his voice has a note of desperation in it I have not heard yet.

"I will not help you," I say.

He pushes my arm away and I move out of his reach.

"You forsake us, Peace-in-the-Sky," he says hoarsely. "You charge us with defending the Tribes-under-the-Dome for all time, and now you abandon us."

"You cannot know my plans or my priorities, Orco." I put my arm around Anissa as she comes to me. "I am leaving now."

"When will you return?" he calls to my back, his voice breaking.

I find the truck Nandi is in. His eyes are wide, and his hands grip the wheel tightly. Anissa climbs in and I fit in beside her. We are squeezed in a row on the bench, and I slam the door behind me.

I reach over Anissa and put my hand on Nandi's arm.

"Nandi? Ready?"

He nods without looking at me and starts the truck, and we drive out into the dawn.

Part 3

The early sun makes us all squint. The light is warm though the windows. Hot, even. Soon it will be painful. But for now, the truck's canopy shields us.

"I don't have any permissions," Nandi says above the sound of the engine. "I'm not sure if we'll get Entry."

"They will let me in," I say.

Nandi gives me a quick glance. "I wasn't any kind of help to you back there."

"Not to worry," I say. I feel weary. No one was killed, I did not violate Dictum 2. I upheld all the Interaction Imperatives. And yet, this is not the way I wish to interact with human societies. It is not the right way to do things.

"Momma can take care of herself," Anissa says. "And me. And you, too, Nandi."

Nandi smiles at her. I turn from both of them and watch the landscape roll by. We are skirting the dome, bumping down a rocky path that leads to the entry point. Nandi says there is no Entry for outsiders at the trade spot. There is only one place where they allow people to apply for admission.

"It's getting hot," Anissa says. "How far, Nandi?"

"Not far. Dipol is the closest post to the Entry. We'll be there before we start to cook."

* * *

I expect a long line, but there's no one visible. We see only a weathered, worn shack with an open porch and a tacked-on veranda to the side, with a dusty truck parked under half of it. We pull in beside it. There are two men on the porch who stand up as they realize our truck is stopping. They jump off the edge of the porch and rush out into position. Both are wearing protective plates on their chests, and they plant their feet and aim bolt-throwing weapons at us.

"Hold!" one shouts.

Both Nandi and Anissa freeze a few paces from the truck, but I keep walking. The two men, who are tall as Tribes-under-the-Dome but also thickly muscular, train their weapons at my chest. I walk up to them and look them in the eyes.

"Peace? Peace-in-the-Sky?" one says.

I reach up and push the end of that one's weapon away from me. He jumps back from my hand. The other keeps his weapon trained on me but steps back uncertainly. I reach behind me for Anissa who comes running up and slips her warm hand in mine. Nandi follows her and we all walk past the two men and up the stairs into the shack.

There's an old woman there standing protectively in front of something concealed by the wide legs of her pants.

"I warn you!" she says loudly before we can speak. "Anyone wanting Entry needs permission chips from the bosses of all five border crews. I won't open the gate for anyone else. No exceptions. I don't care who you are."

"She's Peace-in-the-Sky," says Anissa. "And I'm Riches."

I look out the back door of the shack and see a steel double door set into the side of the dome. There's an electronic control lock sealing it.

"Where's the remote key panel?" I ask the woman.

She frowns. "All three of us have to enter our numbers. Kill any one of us and you'll never get in. You have to get permission chips, or we won't help you."

"I am not going to kill anyone," I say. "But you overreach your authority. Peace-in-the-Sky has permission to enter at any time."

I step around her and see a black metal key panel box on the floor, covered with dust. The men from outside are standing in the doorway. I kneel by the box and the old woman steps away from me reluctantly.

"You need our numbers," she warns me. "You can't guess. If you push too many wrong numbers, it locks for days."

I rub grime from the keypad and key in my code. The display flashes "OVERRIDE" in red and then "ENTRY" in green. There's the sound of a bolt slamming open from the door out back.

The woman looks at me, unsure.

"Sorry to cause you alarm," I say. "Thank you for your work here. It must be a lonely post."

The woman stammers, "Awha, it is. The men switch out every month but I'm always here."

I wave Anissa and Nandi toward the door.

"You're from Tribes-under-the-Dome," I say.

"Only someone who's lived in there understands how important it is to keep it safe."

I see that Nandi and Anissa are waiting by the steel door, their eyes squinted against the brightening light.

"You must miss it," I say.

A sudden flash of pain crosses her face, but she doesn't answer.

"I am sorry," I say. I nod to her, then leave to join Nandi and Anissa.

* * *

Nandi hands out bags with supplies for each of us, then I slide the latch on the control lock. Nandi helps me to pull one of the heavy doors open. Humid fragrant air washes over us and lush leaves unfurl themselves out the door. Anissa cannot contain herself and pushes eagerly through the verdant screen, disappearing immediately. Nandi gives me a nod and then follows. I see only green but I duck my head and push through. Cool leaves brush my face, branches scratch at my legs.

I turn to close the door behind me but the woman from the shack is there, carefully tucking in the greenery and swinging the door shut. There's a resounding clang, then the sound of the bolt shooting closed.

I am hemmed in all around but not concerned. I breathe the air deeply and feel the moisture against my skin as I start to cool after being in the harsh sunlight. I hear Anissa's laughter ahead and push through the brush. There's a path under my feet and I follow it to a shady clearing.

Anissa and Nandi are there, broad smiles on their faces.

"Momma, Momma, Momma!" Anissa leaps at me and throws her arms around me. "You did it! You brought me home. Thank you, thank you, thank you!"

I feel a surge of sharp love for her. I rest my hands on either side of her happy upturned face and press my forehead against hers, eyes closed.

I pull back and look into her eyes "You thank me? Of course I did this for you, Anissa-my-Daughter. What else could I do?"

Nandi is smiling at us, too.

"And thank you, Nandi, for your help," I say.

"Awha, I have not helped you. But I will!" He takes a paper from his bag and unfolds it. I see that it is a hand drawn map. He traces his finger along it.

"We have four days, I think, until we make it to Riches county. Anissa, do you live in Riches capital? Or in a camp?"

"Just outside the capital," Anissa says, looking at the map. She points to an area hesitantly. "Around here."

"Is that map accurate?" I ask Nandi.

He shrugs. "It'll give us an idea. We can ask along the way, too. We'll pass some smaller camps of my Sante tribe."

While we've been standing talking, black long-legged flying insects have been slowly gathering. Anissa slaps at her ankle.

"Skitos," Nandi says, opening his bag. "That's something I haven't missed."

He and Anissa take a pot of some oily paste and smear it on their wrists and ankles and necks.

"Skito balm. Keeps them away. Mostly." Nandi offers the pot to me.

"It's gross!" Anissa says. "You have to eat bananas. If you eat the bananas here, they don't bite so much, and you won't need this stuff." She makes a face at the oily smears on her skin.

I decline the balm. The insects haven't bitten me yet.

I look around us. I can't see further than a few feet into the growth. In comparison to the landscape we just left, this is close and crowded and almost claustrophobic. But I find that I like it. The light is dim, even now that it is full daylight. The dome shades everything, of course, and the canopy of leaves overhead, straining ever upward toward the light, catches much of it. It is shady and cool where we stand.

"Everyone ready?" Nandi asks.

Anissa is bouncing on her toes, eager to set off.

There is a single, narrow path visible under the press of leaves, and Nandi leads us to it. I reach out to push branches away.

"Awha…" Nandi reaches for me tentatively. "Please, treat every tree, every leaf with care. Everything in here belongs to someone and is carefully tended. To harm someone's plants is a terrible crime."

So, we push our way carefully through, slipping by boughs when we can and bending them carefully when necessary. The canopy is high above us, shrubs fill in the understory, and vines wind through it all or creep along the ground. Some plants bear large, brilliant blooms, or tiny green fruits, or long brown pods, or heavy seed heads. Although the foliage is rich and verdant and chaotic, it is clear that the trees are planted in rows and that species are evenly interspersed. The effect is one of a lushly flourishing farm, rather than that of wilderness.

"This is all planted. Everything is food?" I ask.

Anissa sings out, "Cashew nuts and macadamia! Plantains! Coconuts and cacao! Guava and bananas! Yams and taro! Cinnamon and ginger! Turmeric!"

She goes on and I listen to her voice and the quiet chirps of birds and the sound of distant running water. I see some large blue and black butterflies. Life is everywhere, thick and intertwined and woven together at every level.

"I'm so hungry," Anissa says, interrupting her list. "I want to eat right away."

"You know we can't eat from the trees," Nandi tells her. He offers her a strip of dried meat, but she waves it away.

To me he says, "Many people live under the dome and it cannot be expanded to accommodate more, so every scrap of available land is busy growing food to feed them all. And every year people must leave to keep the balance in here. It looks like a bounty, but it is only barely enough."

Anissa is not interested in my education on the matter. "I want tangan stew," she interrupts. "I can't wait! My auntie makes it with black pepper. I like it spicy!"

She turns back to flash me a smile. "You'll like it, too, Momma!"

"If I've had it before, I don't remember it," I say.

I should ask her about where we're going and what my place there is, but I don't. I stop reaching for memories, inwardly turning from the swirl now stirring in my mind. I want to enjoy this trip and the shock of beauty all around us. I don't want to grapple with beam switches, access codes, white corridors, a station in low orbit. Soon I will be home, and whether I can remember it or not now seems unimportant.

I watch the scenery, inhale the scents, breathe the thick air. Always with an eye to Anissa's bobbing head visible through the leaves ahead of me. Anissa-my-Daughter. It is pure joy to watch her bloom in a place where she can be safe, where she doesn't need to be so savvy and shrewd. Here she is simply a happy child.

* * *

It's late in the day when we reach a tidy red clay-walled hut roofed with fronds. There's a clear space around it carpeted in moss. A naked little boy is jumping up and down, singing a song to a bright bird perched on the edge of the roof. Occasionally the bird answers back in trills and warbles, watching the boy with tilted head.

When I stop walking, I feel a wave of nausea and heat wash over me, and it takes me by surprise. It's a moment before my vision clears fully. I swallow several times, stand up straighter and take deep breaths. I stand at the edge of the clearing while Nandi and Anissa approach closer.

Nandi calls out to the hut with a phrase I can't translate, and a woman leans out of the shadowed doorway. They speak for just a moment, and she comes out into the yard and scoops up her child. She is wearing a cloth sheath with a strap over one shoulder. It is dyed in complicated geometric swirls with rich yellows and a deep rust. The woman and the boy are alone.

She and Nandi smile and laugh and gesture, both at ease. I wonder if he knows her, but I remember making that mistake before when Anissa greeted members of the border crew.

Nandi waves a hand in my direction, and the woman stares at me in awe. I incline my head, but she only watches me with a hint of fear in her eyes. When Nandi introduces Anissa, she grins broadly at her and lets her boy down, and he comes running over to Anissa. She squats down and makes faces at him, and he laughs and pulls at her hair.

"She says we can camp here," Nandi says, coming over to where I wait. "She'll feed Anissa, and I told her I have food for myself, but she wonders if you need to eat." He adds quietly, "Every morsel of food here is so important."

"I will eat only what is left that she can spare," I say.

We walk over to the woman and Nandi relays this in their dialect. It is similar to the crew's and to Anissa's dialect, and yet still subtly different.

Then we sit, and it's a relief to rest my legs and my throbbing head. Perhaps I should have been drinking more as we walked. I drink now from a clay bowl the woman gave us and feel some relief.

Nandi sits with me, and we watch Anissa and the boy play.

I wave a fat buzzing insect away from my head and Nandi looks at me, concerned.

"Look in your bag," he tells me.

There is a pot of skito balm, some strips of dried meat, and a colorful swath of cloth.

"You can cover your head," Nandi says. "Tie it like this." He holds his arms up and mimics wrapping it around.

I wrap it loosely and then tuck the ends in carefully.

"That will keep the bugs from getting to it," Nandi says. "Tie it tighter if you have to. You don't want them getting in there and eating away at it." He shudders.

* * *

Later two men come home, one I take to be the woman's husband and the other must be an older relative. Nandi embraces the men like they are brothers, and they talk and laugh loudly. When they see me, their expressions become more guarded, and they ask Nandi quiet questions.

I listen to the men talking as closely as I can, waiting for the intricacies of their dialect to become clear to me. By the time the woman comes out of the hut carrying a bowl on either hip, I understand them well.

Anissa and the boy rush over and chorus "thank you, Momma," as she sets down the food. The adults watch the children eat greedily with patient smiles, then they begin to eat.

Nandi asks them about every person he once knew and gets from them all the news they have, and now their conversation turns to what prices may be had in the market for various wares. The woman hands me one of the bowls with some food left in the bottom. It's sweet and dense, a root cooked to tenderness in some highly seasoned sauce. The taste is complex, far from the simple foods we had outside the dome. If Anissa was accustomed to this, she must have found our other food bland.

After the meal the older man pulls two mangoes from his bag and cuts slices for us all.

"For this occasion," he says, nodding at me solemnly. "Welcome, welcome, Peace-in-the-Sky."

"Thank you," I say.

The light fades and the family goes inside their hut to sleep, while we travelers stretch ourselves out on the mossy lawn. Nandi swats skitos. The air is thick with them. Anissa smears more balm on her ankles and wrists and curls up against me, resting her head on my arm.

*　*　*

She wakes me early in the morning. Birds are calling all around us. I lay on my back looking up at the pattern of leaves above us. They are many shades of green, brown, and burgundy, all interleaved in a peaceful patchwork bright with the morning sunlight behind it all.

For breakfast there is a warm drink Anissa is excited about, and she gives me a sip of hers. It has a rich, bittersweet taste and it's thick enough to eat with a spoon.

"Atole," she whispers with an excited smile. "It's made with cacao."

I hand her small cup back to her and she drinks it slowly, eyes half-closed.

Nandi embraces everyone as we prepare to set out, and Anissa hugs the little boy, and we get underway. It is a long day of walking, but the pace is easy. Anissa and I have been accustomed to walking, it is Nandi who calls a stop.

"My feet!" He sits down to rub them with a laugh. "I ride in the truck too much in my new life."

We all sit.

"Is it nice being back, Nandi?" I ask. "Or is it hard?"

He laughs. "It is both. I didn't want to leave the first time, and when I have to leave here again, it will be hard again."

"I am sorry I brought you here," I say.

"No! I'm grateful to visit! I may never have had the chance again."

"You would have been separated from your family forever?" I ask.

"Oh, they may come to visit sometimes, at the trade spot. But the crew is supposed to be my family, now. That's what we must do, to keep the Preserve. The sacrosanct, the plenitude, the prospect."

He waits for me to say something, but I don't know what he expects.

* * *

We find a group of clay huts late in the afternoon and decide to cut our day short. They are Nandi's tribe again, the Sante, and they know him. They plan a gathering, and some people walk over from other camps, so that by evening there's a large group and lots of food. Always just enough for everyone to eat well, but not more. Anissa eats heartily and I'm grateful for their generosity to her. It's always a pleasure to see her nourished. Nandi embraces each newcomer and sheds tears, and they tell stories and answer his eager questions.

I sit away from the crowd. As it grows late, Anissa brings me a little food she wants me to try and sits with me. I eat, and she leans her head on my arm. When I finish, I wrap my arm around her.

"You are missing home," I say.

She wipes tears away.

"I'm happy for Nandi," she says.

I feel proud that she can put aside what she has wanted for so long to see how nice this is for him.

"I am, too," I say. "It would be good if he could see his parents again."

"But we can't travel to the Sante capital," Anissa says, looking at me. "It's too far out of the way."

"We will go home first, Anissa. Then Nandi may have some time to visit his home before returning to the crew."

"He's not supposed to do that," she says. "Once you leave Tribes-under-the-Dome, you don't return."

"Don't you want me to change things to make it easier for Nandi?" I ask her.

"No. Well, yes, Nandi is nice. I like his smile. I wish he was my brother," Anissa says thoughtfully. "But it's so important to keep Tribes-under-the-Dome in and the Intha out. Otherwise..." Her face twists sadly. "Otherwise, the Intha will take everything."

Her words settle on me heavily. "Ask Nandi to come to me," I tell her.

She looks at me with a worried expression. "Did I get him in trouble, Momma?"

"No, no."

She gets up and walks back to the crowd, giving me a backward glance.

A few moments later Nandi joins me. He is flushed with the excitement of the night, cheeks round and reddened, with a broad smile that touches every part of his face.

"Nandi, we are glad you have this gathering tonight. It must be good to see people you know."

His smile fades. "It's making Anissa's heart ache for her family," he says.

"It is. But we will see them soon. Is it possible to reach her Riches tribe tomorrow?" It is not only Anissa's desire that drives me, but fear over my deteriorating injury. I wish to have her somewhere safe before I am no longer able to travel.

Nandi pulls out his map.

"A long walk," he says, "especially since we stopped early today."

"Maybe if you had something to cover your feet."

"They could make me something from layers of plantain leaves. But even the leaves are so valuable. They break down to make the rich dirt needed to grow everything. I don't dare ask."

"I will ask them," I say.

Nandi looks uncomfortable. "You could speak to Veras. She's the elder mother here."

"Send her to me so that I can thank her," I say. "We leave early tomorrow, Nandi. With lots of ground to cover before dark. But enjoy yourself tonight."

"I will," he says.

When Veras comes I ask her to sit with me. She squats near me. There is no fear on her face, but she is wary. For the first time I speak their dialect.

"Thank you, Veras, for taking care of us and for welcoming back Nandi with such a happy gathering."

Her wariness fades and she smiles. "He is kin! My cousin's husband's nephew. Not our blood, but our family, all the same. And thank you, Peace-in-the-Sky, for honoring us with your visit. I have never seen you, but my childhood was full of stories of all the things you did for Sante and all Tribes-under-the-Dome."

"Maybe you will repay me with a small favor. We have far to go, and we must move quickly. Nandi is our guide, but his feet grow weary. Do you have anything for him?"

Veras looks surprised. "Does he need sandals?"

"If there're some you can spare," I say. "And some food for his journey."

"Alright," she says. She seems confused but not angry. "We diligently conserve our crops. For our future, the one you have promised us, we do keep the Preserve. The sacrosanct, the plenitude, the prospect."

"I am not testing you," I say. "I am sure that you do. I'm asking you to bend the rules because of the necessity of my journey. And I don't visit often."

She nods. "It is true."

"Thank you," I tell her.

* * *

We wake very early. I set the pace this time. By now I am more practiced at slipping past the foliage without damaging it, so I push us to go quickly. Anissa trots excitedly behind me, and Nandi keeps up with us and does not complain.

My head aches. My scalp and face are burning with an internal heat. I loosen my headwrap, but it doesn't help. I drink deeply each time we stop. I don't want to turn inward because of the effort it takes, but I'm forced to so I can divert more energy to physical function. I must keep walking.

A thick fog passes us, and moisture beads up on our skin and drips from the leaves all around us. Little puddles form in the cups of dried leaves on the forest floor, and rivulets run among the roots, finding streams to join. When we hear sounds of human habitation, we conclude that a settlement is nearby, but we can see nothing, so we push on through the fog.

By the time it lifts Anissa has begun to recognize the area. She chooses our paths, though Nandi still consults his map. Day has faded to afternoon, and we push ahead faster and faster. A few times I reach out to tree trunks to steady myself. I fight vertigo.

Finally, Anissa gives a happy cry. I look up and try to focus, as my vision has narrowed to a small field.

* * *

The homes of the Riches tribe are clay like the others we have seen, but they are less squat, with more windows and wider doorways. The roofs are fashioned from halved bamboo shafts arranged neatly in multiple layers that collect water and guide it to tubs under the eaves. In front are narrow beds of flowering plants that attract showy butterflies and buzzing bees. Behind are neat gardens, delineated with string, that grow bunches of small red fruits and herb bushes of many kinds. There are narrow paths all around the houses and throughout the settlement worn deep into the dirt. The forest crop crowds all around, divided into parcels marked with brightly colored string that winds its way through the understory, looped loosely over branches to keep it up out of the dirt.

We pass mostly women and children, who stare openly. Little boys wear un-dyed skirts of brown cloth, but the women wear an intense bright red that sets them off from the greenery around them.

Despite our long, hard march Anissa is bouncing with excitement. She speeds down the path ahead of us, leading the way. Nandi stops to exchange some words with onlookers, and they gasp and clap in excitement. Some run ahead, maybe to bring news of our arrival. Before long, we attract a crowd that follows along with us. I know their language already. It is Anissa's and I have been speaking it since I first woke in that swinging cage among the Intha.

Many in the crowd reach out to Anissa, patting her head, squeezing her hand, and she has smiles for them all, but she presses forward. Our path takes a turn, and the way opens up to another small group of huts. Hustling down the path to meet us are a group of women of all ages, and children around them in a cloud.

In the lead is a woman who has both hands pressed over her mouth.

Anissa screams and sprints forward.

She collides with the woman, and they wrap their arms tightly around each other. The woman sobs painfully and Anissa cries on her shoulder. The other women surround them and some of them cry as well. Others shout joyfully and the children bounce and jump and pull at their mothers.

I stop.

The crowd behind us surges forward and around me, and joins the celebrating group, and I see only the backs of those on the margins.

After a few minutes, I feel Nandi at my elbow. He must have stayed behind with me.

"Peace-in-the-Sky?" he asks carefully.

I don't answer.

"Are you upset? You must have known..."

I hold up my hand to stop him talking.

He hovers nervously.

We stand that way for a long time.

And then the celebrating crowd is thinning. Anissa's story has been told and heard. Joyful songs and little dances that arose spontaneously are over. People are walking back to their homes, wiping their eyes of tears, carrying their children. Some of them pause to stare at the unusual sight of a Peace-in-the-Sky, if they even recognize me for what I am with my hair nearly covered. But none approach me.

I see the woman again, and she has her arm tight around Anissa. She looks at me, and Anissa glances in my direction but her eyes slide from mine guiltily. Their faces are pressed closely so that I cannot hear their conversation at this distance. The woman pushes Anissa firmly into the arms of a nearby relative, who pulls the protesting Anissa away to what must be their home.

The woman approaches me. Her eyes dance back and forth between me and Nandi.

I wait motionless as she walks. I see her simultaneously as a red hash on a map and as herself. I see her thick, dark hair, where mine is colorless. I see she has breasts to nurse a baby. As I do not.

She stops at a distance from me, pauses for just a moment, then gets down on her knees and spreads her arms out in front of her, pressing her face into the ground. The dispersing crowd pauses and some groups watch us. I can see their confusion.

"Peace-in-the-Sky!" the woman says at last, raising her head. "Godshard!"

Anyone watching is now silent.

"Let her speak," Nandi says quietly. "Let her come closer."

I don't say anything, but after a moment Nandi calls to the woman, "Come speak to her."

The woman gets up and halves the distance between us before kneeling again.

She looks up at me with tears and dirt all over her cheeks. I see the arch of her eyebrows, the rounded chin, the shape of her bottom lip. All familiar to me.

"Peace-in-the-Sky, you returned to me that which I love most. She whom I cannot replace. Anissa is my heart and my joy and my life. No favor I can do for you will ever equal this favor."

She waits, but I say nothing. I am frozen in place.

"Anissa tells me that you...traveled together." The woman looks at Nandi nervously, then back to me. "She may have said things that...don't ring true. Understand, ever since she was little that one was so very, very clever. She could tell a story so smoothly. Maybe I should have raised her differently, but it was so delightful to see her cleverness. And now I hear that even when she was so far from us and so hopeless, somehow, she found her bold words. And it has saved her."

She pauses again for me to respond. I am utterly, unblinkingly still.

"Please forgive her anything she's done. She's only a child. And she had no one to help her." A few tears run down the woman's face. "Anything that's mine I give you, anything I can do for you, I will do it. Come stay in my home, it's yours as much as mine. Let's celebrate together, all three?"

When the moments stretch out and I still don't answer, she and Nandi shift anxiously, exchange glances, look to me again.

"Please. Come whenever you'd like. Thank you, thank you."

She presses her face to the ground again, then gets up and backs away, smiling through her tears. She turns and goes back to her hut where relatives run to embrace her. She sends one last look over her shoulder before she's drawn inside and there's the sound of excited shouting and happy crying. Before long the smell of cooking fires is everywhere, and there are pots banging and people talking and laughing in every hut.

Nandi still stands just out of my field of view to the right.

"Peace-in-the-Sky? Are you alright?"

I turn and leave the path, walk to the edge of the forest, and sit with my back to a wide tree there. Nandi sits beside me.

"Are you broken?" he asks quietly. "Can you speak?"

"I can speak," I say. My throat is dry.

"I'm sorry you found out like this. I thought you knew. I thought you surely must know."

I don't answer him. Because I did know. I knew all was not as it seemed. But I had held onto hope that there was so much I did not understand, that perhaps when all was made clear I would still find Anissa-my-Daughter in my arms.

We sit until it begins to get dark. My ears ring with the pain in my head. People sometimes pass us on the path and smile or nod before continuing. Many of them are going to visit Anissa's hut.

"Can I help you somehow?" Nandi asks. "What can I do?"

"There is nothing," I say.

"Can I put my arm around you?"

"No."

He waits longer and I say nothing. Skitos gather one by one and circle us lazily.

"Awha, Peace-in-the-Sky, how can I serve you? You scare me."

I turn to look at him.

He gives a little exhale of relief. "What comforts you? We could slide together." There's a little laugh in his voice as he says it.

I feel a surge of irritation in all the emptiness I am drowning in.

"Are you offering sexual intercourse?" I ask.

Nandi laughs warmly, only a little abashed.

"This shell is androgyne. It's not equipped for that," I say.

The smile on his face slides away. "You're wearing a shell?"

"This is a shell," I say.

"It's not your body?"

"No."

"But...where is your body, then?"

"Dead," I say. "Long dead."

Nandi lapses into confused silence.

After a moment he says, "I got you to talk again."

"Nandi, go. Join their celebration. Go enjoy yourself."

"No, I'm sticking by you." He leans against the tree I lean on, his arm brushes against mine.

He smears his ankles with skito balm, then pulls some food from his pack. Offers me some, but begins to eat when I shake my head.

As it grows dark an old man walks cautiously over to us.

"Come stay with us?" he asks. "My old wife invites you. We have a sleeping mat for you, even. Our two younger sons left not long ago for the border crew in Sas Tabo."

"Thank you," Nandi tells him.

He stands and offers me his hand, but I can stand without help.

The inside of the hut is cool and black. I augment my sight with infrared as Nandi and I find the sleeping mat they have laid out for us in the main room. There's another room behind it, and the old couple disappear into there for the night.

We lay down on a mat woven from grasses and worn thin and soft with use. Nandi puts his arms around me from behind and pulls me close. I am numb. I am here, but I don't feel present.

"Nandi, I am going to sleep now," I tell him. "You must wake me in the morning. I can't wake myself."

"Alright," he says.

* * *

It's not him that wakes me, though, it's the old woman. She comes into the room and starts to quietly prepare food. Nandi is asleep behind me. For a moment I mistake his arms, his warmth, his quiet breath for Anissa's presence. I swallow and it feels like I'm trying to swallow cold scraps of metal. The side of my face is burning hot.

I ease away from Nandi and stand up.

The old woman steals glances at me but won't look me in the eye. I walk to the wall of the hut where there is an old mirror hung. It's cloudy and some spots are flaked away. I unwind the cloth from my head and turn so that I can see my wound. It's crusted over and mostly dry now, my white hair caked into the mess.

I reach up and try to scrape some of the gore away with my fingernail. Alarms go off inside my head, but I silence them. Then there's only the pain to deal with. I pick away dried blood and fluid and underneath find angry red flesh, inflamed and rotting. Outwardly the wound is healing over, but within it is festering. This wet climate is accelerating things.

Then I search deeper. I get my nail under the edge of a piece of cracked bone, a fragment of skull that is held in place only by dried fluids. I pry up the sticky edge.

The alarms, heard only inwardly by me, blare so deafeningly I can hear nothing else. Red warning pulses obscure my vision.

But I enhance my sight and, during the brief periods of clear vision I have, I inspect the pink matter under the skull fragment. I enhance my sight again and again. Through the red flashes, despite the poor light in the hut and the clouded mirror, I glimpse sparkling filaments running through the brain tissue. I wretch violently, though I have nothing in my stomach.

I take my hand away and let the piece of skull move wetly back into place. The alarms are dampened, and my vision slowly clears. The pain is still there. It will take longer to subside.

I take deep even breaths. I gently wind the cloth around my head again. If only I had looked when Orco showed me his mirror, maybe I would have been prepared for yesterday. If I had truly thought critically about myself...but then I was always thinking about Anissa. Thinking about getting her home. I had put aside every other line of inquiry to be dealt with after Anissa was safe.

I walk to the door of the hut and look out into the morning. Mist and the smoke from cooking fires mingle to obscure the other huts and the pathway and even the encroaching forest, which appears as a hazy, even green. I look to my left. Down the path that way lies Anissa's hut. I cannot make it out clearly.

I watch that way for a long time.

"Peace-in-the-Sky?" Nandi asks quietly.

I turn away from the door. The old woman has set out some food on a bench, and everyone is gathering to squat around it.

"Come eat a little," Nandi says.

I go and sit with them, but I don't eat. They eat and talk quietly and send me glances from the side of their eyes. The old woman is curious. The old man is cautious. And Nandi is concerned.

When they are done the old man clears away the clay bowls.

I walk to the door again. The mist is clearing. Men of all ages with bags and tools over their shoulders are dispersing into the surrounding forest, following footpaths that are visible only as they part the leaves. Some carry young children on their shoulders.

"We can go and visit later this morning," Nandi says. He's come to stand just behind me.

"Visit?"

"Go to see Anissa, and her family."

I feel like I've been struck. It's a moment before I can reply.

"No."

"No?" Nandi asks. "You want to give them a day or so, first?"

"No."

"What are you saying?"

"We set out this morning, Nandi. I need a clear view to the sky. Find us the fastest way out from under the dome."

"What?" Nandi turns to look at me.

"This shell is dying."

"Awha! What will happen?"

"I need to return to the station. If this shell dies with me in it, I also die."

"What about Anissa? You should at least say good-bye to her."

The smell of Anissa's hair suddenly returns to me. I almost reach out to touch her. But she isn't there.

"No. I need to leave," I say.

"Just leave? But you can make time for this one thing."

I turn away from him.

"Peace-in-the-Sky? I don't understand you. You called her your daughter and you believed it, right? You really believed it? And now you want to just leave her?"

Anissa, huddled under my arm with her eyes squeezed shut. Anissa running ahead of me and laughing. Anissa curled up warm beside me at night. Anissa's voice calling me "momma."

"Peace-in-the-Sky?" Nandi prods.

"The quickest way out from under the dome. I need an unobstructed view of the sky."

Confusion in his voice, Nandi says, "At the height of the dome are air cleaners that vent to the sky. If you're desperate you could go there. Climb the ladder. There're locks but I bet you can open them."

"You'll guide me?"

He laughs in surprise. "You're really going to do it? Yes, alright. I'll guide you. I do what you say, don't I? You're Peace-in-the-Sky."

I turn my head and for a moment we look at each other.

"I'm sorry," he says. "I can't understand you. You're a god, really, aren't you? Though they tell us over and over again that you are not. And your face is like a mask. But I will help you."

"My face *is* a mask," I tell him. "And thank you."

It takes Nandi only a few moments to prepare. He studies his map, gathers our bags and drinks, borrows a strigil to scrape away the stale skito balm. He thanks the old couple but tells them nothing about our plans, and we leave.

It is full daylight, and warm and humid. Women are emerging from their huts to carry water and tend the gardens. Children play in the open spaces, racing each other down the narrow paths.

But we turn between two huts and the forest swallows us. Happy sounds from the settlement fade behind us. I strain to hear Anissa's voice one last time, but I cannot.

Anissa. The soft feel of her skin. Her small hand with long, narrow fingers clasped in mine. Her tiny pink fingernails against her dark skin. I stop walking.

Nandi stops, too. "Are you alright?"

After a moment of silence I say, "I am not well."

Nandi says, "Let me carry your bag."

It is almost empty anyway, and he folds it up and tucks it in his.

I start walking again and Nandi walks behind me, letting me set the pace. Every step is an effort. Leaves brush my face. We pass near someone working in the forest, though not close enough to see. We hear the rustling of dry leaves and the chipping sound of a tool against wood. We walk on and the sounds fade. Chip, chip, chip.

Anissa, Anissa, Anissa. I will never see her again. It would be nearly impossible to return in the time frame of her life span.

I stumble on a rock and fall to one knee.

"Peace!" Nandi jumps forward, reaches out to me, hesitates, then takes my arm and helps me to my feet.

He peers at me anxiously. "You look ashen in the face," he says.

I will never see her grown to a woman. I will never see her children.

"Peace, can you walk?"

"I can."

I set my foot on the path. It is only wide enough for one foot at a time.

Nandi follows close behind me.

Noon approaches and our pace has slowed to a halting walk. The heat in my face is like a fire.

"Peace-in-the-Sky, what is wrong?" Nandi asks when we stop to drink. "Are you dying? Is your heart breaking?"

"I don't know myself," I say, and my voice sounds whispery to me. I drink more. "Perhaps it is both."

I want to lie down, but I'm afraid to lose consciousness.

"But if you get back," Nandi says worriedly, "you can be fixed, right?"

"My consciousness will be transferred to another shell," I say. I lean my elbow on a moss-covered rock. I'm too tired to search for words that will be more meaningful for him. And I'm still myself processing all the memories that are leaking back—disjointed, disordered, disquieting.

"You get...another body? And you'll be okay, right? You've done it before?"

"Hundreds of times."

"And you'll still remember things?"

Anissa. Coming to shelter under my arm from the torment of the Intha. Feeling her start to feel safe.

"Yes." I start to slide away from the rock.

Nandi leans forward and offers his hand.

"I will carry you there," he says. "But will you be able to make the climb? It's a long, long ladder."

"I don't know," I say. "But Nandi, you cannot carry me through this underbrush. The path is too narrow."

"Parents carry their children, don't they? My own father carried me on his shoulder so that I could help him work our crops."

"You yourself are tired and worn," I say.

"For you, I will make a mighty effort," Nandi says, his smile broad.

I like him. Very much. I like all of them. The crowded Tribes-under-the-Dome, the pushy border crews, the Intha violent in their desperation for survival. I cannot help it. It is part of my design.

"I will shut down all but the most essential functions," I tell him. "I may appear dead. When we arrive at the ladder you must wake me."

"Awha, how?" he asks. "I'm afraid to be rough with you. I'm afraid to even carry you when you're not awake to know it's just me. You can still call the pillars-of-flame."

"Perhaps," I say. "Try making a loud noise close to my ear, or pulling back my eyelid."

"It scares me when you talk about things uncertainly," he says. "If you don't know, who does?"

I drink again and again. I am so thirsty.

"Ready?" Nandi asks.

"Yes," I say. He takes my arm and bends down to pull me across his shoulders. My head swims as he stands, and I start shutting down while I can still control myself. The gentle rocking of Nandi's plodding gait lulls me and then, all at once, everything is gone.

* * *

A pulsing blue light in my vision. Then Nandi's face above mine. He looks hot and weary.

Then there is sound, too.

Running water. A bird calling.

"Are you back with me?" Nandi asks.

I sit up.

"Yes," I say.

This shell still lives. I am somewhat rested. Behind Nandi I see a stainless-steel ladder glinting among the leaves.

Nandi sits beside me. "It took me a while to find it. A narrow ladder in all this." He gestures around to the greenery. "I had to set you down and climb a tree to see above the canopy and spot it. Climb a tree! I clambered over someone else's tree."

"Thank you," I say. "I know it's taboo for you."

"Because Peace-in-the-Sky says it is," he says. "So, I thought, for you I could do it."

"Thank you. But I only said that resources must be carefully conserved. It was Tribes-under-the-Dome who carved the forest into pieces for the exclusive use of each family."

We walk to a nearby stream and drink. I am still thirsty, but it is not the desperate ache it was before. I splash water on my face.

"Are you still thinking of climbing?" Nandi asks.

"Yes. Though I need fuel for the effort." I reach out into the bushes and break off the tender ends of branches, and chew them.

Nandi watches me with wide eyes. "What will the man think when he comes and sees his foliage like this?"

"When I have gone up," I say, "I want you to leave. Go see your family. Ask your mother to feed you. Stay for a while and visit."

"I would never ask Mam to break with the Preserve," Nandi says.

I tear up handfuls of some low-growing legume and eat it, leaves, stems, roots and all.

"You are hers; she will feed you. I would instruct you to remain with your Sante tribe for the rest of your life, but I don't think there's a place for you there anymore."

"Awha! Why are you doing this for me?" Nandi asks.

"I want to repay you," I say. "Or, more truthfully, I want a better life for you." I want a better life for all of them, though I am in no shape to aid them. There are many, many injustices in their world, and it pains me that so many are upheld by traditions established by Peace-in-the-Sky.

Nandi just watches me silently while I eat a handful of hard, dark berries.

"Those aren't for eating," he says.

"It doesn't matter," I say.

We go to stand by the ladder.

"Will I see you again?" he asks me as I look up.

The ladder extends far, far up until it disappears into the thickness of the air.

"No," I say. "Given the damage to this shell, and the difficulty of coordinating any trip, it's unlikely that I could return in your lifetime. Even assuming that my trip is approved, which is even less likely."

Anissa. I see her peaceful, sleeping face. There's a pounding ache in my chest.

"What will I tell Boss?" Nandi asks. A question directed more to himself, but I answer anyway.

"Tell him that I was impressed by his need and moved by his plight. Tell him I am thankful for his gift of your guidance under the dome. Tell him I will return in the time of his successor to repair the dome."

"Is that true?"

"No. Or, at least, I doubt that it will be."

Nandi sighs and looks sad. I wait for him to ask me what his people should do. I wait for him to ask for guidance and direction and hope. I wait for him to ask for prophecy.

But he doesn't. It's not in Nandi's nature to grapple with the larger concerns. He sees only the people around him and his relationships with those he cares about. And I do not fool myself that any hasty parting instructions could cause meaningful change. There is too much to be done here, and I find myself too broken to be useful. Just as Rill said.

"Is there anything else I can do for you before I go?" I ask.

He meets my eyes and his smile returns.

"I'll miss you," he says. "I wanted to figure you out, but I guess I won't."

"No."

"It's too much to think I might be the man who slides together with a god." He smiles his reluctant smile. "But can I have a kiss? I'd remember it the rest of my life."

I feel a familiar stab of irritation, this time tempered with forbearance.

"If you wish."

He hesitates for a moment, steps closer, and touches his lips softly to mine. Then leans back and looks into my eyes.

He laughs nervously. "I guess I'll never see you smile, either."

"If it makes any difference," I say, "I do smile. But the nerve impulses are blocked from changing the muscles in my face."

He laughs. "Awha, that I really do not understand."

"Good-bye, Nandi," I say. "Thank you."

"Peace-in-the-Sky," he says solemnly.

I look up. And I start to climb.

* * *

By the time I rise above the canopy, I am exhausted. Nausea, chills, a burning ache in my head and neck. I am not as recovered as I hoped. I climb a while more and pause to look down. The treetops look like a verdant, rolling field. The heat from the sun above, even filtered through the dome, is growing. The air is becoming thick with the smoke being gathered into the filters high above me. I hyperventilate to saturate my blood with oxygen in case respiration becomes difficult.

Then I selectively choose all non-essential processes to shut down. I stop biologically necessary functions knowing it will kill this shell. I am now dying. I have several hours. And in those hours, I need to make this climb, reach the top, activate my beacon, and return to the station. And if the shell dies? This hole in my heart where Anissa once lived will cease to cause me such pain.

I close my eyes and imagine I rest my cheek against Anissa's smooth cheek. I breathe in the smell that is her and only her. And I climb.

ACKNOWLEDGEMENTS

I would not be a writer without my writers' group. They nurtured and encouraged me, and I'm so grateful to have found a community with them where I could grow and learn. Blakely Lord, K.D. Edwards, Scott Reintgen, Ali Standish, Paige Nguyen, Kwame Mbalia, Caitlin Coons, Jennifer Perez, Tyler Ellzey, and many others who came and went: thank you.

Thank you to William C. Tracy, and the team at Space Wizard Science Fantasy, who took a chance on an untried author and helped me learn the process of getting a book published.

ABOUT THE AUTHOR

Caye Marsh is a former biologist writing Sci-Fi and Fantasy. She cherishes the unbroken quiet of wild places and the true dark of night, so please keep it down and remember to extinguish all outdoor lights. You can find her at cayemarsh.com.

Please take a moment to review this book at your favorite retailer's website, Goodreads, or simply tell your friends!